A *Just Cause Universe* Novel

Ian Thomas Healy

Local Hero Press Edition

The Neighborhood Watch
A *Just Cause Universe* Novel
Published by Local Hero Press, LLC

1st Printing
Local Hero Press: trade paperback, September 1, 2016
Printed in the United States of America

ISBN-13: 9781971445991

Cover art by Karyn Lewis Bonfiglio
Book design by Local Hero Press, LLC

Books by Local Hero Press

The *Just Cause Universe*

Just Cause
The Archmage
Day of the Destroyer
Deep Six
Jackrabbit
Champion
Castles
The Lion and the Five Deadly Serpents
Tusks
The Neighborhood Watch
Jackrabbit: Big In Japan
Arena
Hero Academy
The Path
Cinco de Mayo
Search and Rescue
Rooftops
Plague
Soldiers of Fortune
Just Cause Universe Compendium
Destroyer of Earth
Flint and Steel
The Club
Jackrabbit: Rinse and Repeat
Posse
Extinction Event
Rain Must Fall

Pariah of Verigo

Pariah's Moon
Pariah's War

Three Flavors of Tacos

The Guitarist
Making the Cut
The Scene Stealers

Collections

Airship Lies
High Contrast
The Good Fight
The Good Fight 3: Sidekicks
The Good Fight 4: Homefront
The Good Fight 5: The Golden Age
Muddy Creek Tales
Caped

Other Novels

Assassin
Blood on the Ice
Funeral Games
Hope and Undead Elvis
Horde
The Murder Squad (2026)
Roast Wyvern (and Other Recipes)
Starf*cker
Strings
The Oilman's Daughter
Troubleshooters

Nonfiction

Action! Writing Better Action Using Cinematic Techniques

For Fillip—the first Rascal

I always have so many people to thank when there's a new Just Cause Universe book to bring out to the world. Many thanks are due my regular editor and dear friend Allison M. Dickson, and equally dear friend and partner-in-crime Alicia Howie. I can't say enough about artist Karyn Lewis Bonfiglio's beautiful work except that there isn't enough of it in the world. I'm especially grateful to my family—yes, even my obnoxious teenage children—for providing so much of the inspiration to write this book. Finally, I must thank all the parents who have come to see me at conventions and sadly left empty-handed because I didn't have a book for their younger readers. This one's for you. I hope you enjoy it!

Ian Thomas Healy
August, 2016

Chapter One

May, 2018
Loveland, Colorado

When the alarm on her phone went off, Annalisa Torres was trying on her new costume.

It wasn't easy, being the leader of a team of youthful superheroes who were all too young to attend the Hero Academy in Denver. Well, she was only sort of the leader. Wheels was much better at that sort of thing. She had all her gimmicks and tools and everything that almost made up for being in a wheelchair. Wheels was probably the group's actual leader, but Annalisa could fly, and she had the most heroic-sounding super name of the team, so that was something.

She'd had a long argument with Hothead about her name: *La Capitána*. He said she should be Captain *Something*. That was a better name, he said, a heroic name. She thought it over, and tried out several different Captain *Whatevers*, but none of them sounded as good in her ears as La Capitána, so that's what she was going to be.

At the moment her phone began beeping like an overexcited bird, Annalisa was posing in her bedroom. She was hovering over her bed in her green t-shirt with the white star and jean shorts that were maybe a little too big. She had a belt to hold them up, and she called it her *utility belt*, so that was okay. On her feet were the big clunky boots that belonged to her mom, and across her shoulders, of course, her red cape.

The others were always asking her about the cape. Why would she wear it at all? It was just going to get caught or tangled in stuff, or a supervillain might grab hold of it and play tetherball with her head using it. But the others just didn't understand. Capes *looked* cool, and as long as La Capitána was part of the Neighborhood Watch, she was going to try to look as cool as she could.

At least Breezy understood. He had a cape. Of course, he needed his to fly, because he used it like a reverse parachute with his air control powers. His always looked pretty cool, the way it filled up with air and lifted him into the sky.

Annalisa dropped onto her bed with a satisfying thump and snagged her phone as it bounced away from the covers. The app Wheels had written was making the screen flash with a scan of the Neighborhood Watch logo. Rascal had drawn for them. He was the best artist of the team, but Annalisa thought that was because he was always tagging stuff with a fat Sharpie he kept in his pocket for just such an eventuality. He was a super-powered skateboarder, which didn't make any sense until you saw him using his powers, at which point you got it. She swiped away the logo and read the text from Wheels beneath it.

Emergency! Convene at HQ for debriefing ASAP! Plz respond!

Annalisa shook her head. Wheels was always using fancy terms like *debriefing* when nobody but her knew what they meant. For that matter, Annalisa suspected Wheels might not know what they really meant either, but she delighted in sounding important. Still, being a superhero— even at twelve years old—meant one had to put aside one's desires when it came to duty, and right now, duty was calling. Annalisa pecked out *capitana on my way* without bothering with such niceties as spelling, punctuation, or language-appropriate accents.

She opened her window, letting the early summer breeze swirl around her bedroom, making posters on the walls flutter. Annalisa reminded herself she needed to close the window behind her. More than once she'd flown off and left it open, oblivious to any negative effects until her mom yelled at her about the electric bill.

Her parents knew about her powers. Although it wasn't common for kids to develop parahuman abilities before puberty, it wasn't unheard-of, either. Annalisa had been able to fly since elementary school, and it had been difficult for her to understand that no, not everybody else could do it. Nor could everyone else pick up a car. Super-strength, super-toughness, and flight weren't uncommon powers as far as parahuman abilities went, but that didn't matter to her. In two years she'd be fourteen and starting her first year at Just Cause's Hero Academy. After that, well, she could go anywhere. Every superhero team needed a good flying brick—that's what the internet called people like her—but Annalisa didn't want to be on just *any* team. She wanted to be on the Big One. The One that Mattered.

Just Cause New York!

She was kind of obsessed with the New York team. Some kids were into bands and sports teams, but not Annalisa. She was into parahumans. She hit up the Just Cause website several times a day, followed the heroes and teams on social media, and participated in forums under her hero name La Capitána, even though she wasn't *technically* old enough to do so.

"Hey, Capitána, wait up!" A brown-skinned boy with short dreadlocks flew up to join her from a nearby street, his winds inflating his large blue cape and lifting him aloft.

"Hey, Breezy." Annalisa smiled at him and he grinned back. His real name was Bryson but he hated it so much that he'd been going by Breezy since Kindergarten. She noticed his costume, or more specifically, his lack of it. He had his cape, but besides that wore a tank top and basketball shorts instead of the swirly-white bodysuit his mom had bought for him on the internet. "What's the matter, is it laundry day?"

"It's Sunday. Ain't it supposed to be our day off?"

"Crime doesn't take days off. Neither should we."

"Besides, where's your costume?"

Annalisa wanted to smack him, but as strong as she was, she might actually hurt him. "I'm wearing it, stupid."

"It's different. I thought you were goin' to wear that gymnastics leotard."

She rolled her eyes. "Nobody wears stuff like that when they're being superheroes. They all have super-expensive high-tech polymers in their costumes. Like Kevlar nanoweave."

Breezy shrugged. "I dunno what that is. But I don't think nobody wears jean shorts and a t-shirt to be a superhero neither."

"That's not true. Bombshell does. She's super-strong like me but she can't fly and I can." Annalisa did a barrel roll just because she could.

Breezy giggled. "I'm just messin' with ya. I don't care what kinda costume you wear."

"You . . . you jerk!" Annalisa dove beneath him, grabbed one of his feet, and turned him upside down.

"Hey! Hey, quit it! I can't fly when I'm like this!" Breezy shrieked loud enough to make a couple of people walking on the street below look up in surprise. "Dang it, Annie, stop it!"

Annalisa turned him right-side up again and waited until his cape inflated before letting go. "Don't call me Annie . . . *Bryson*."

Breezy laughed and blew a puff of air right into Annalisa's face. "Gotcha. Hey, look, there's Hothead."

Annalisa looked down and saw a bicyclist standing on his pedals, pumping hard like his hair was on fire.

His hair really *was* on fire.

Hothead's name was Cole, and he was an angry boy. His anger manifested as parts of him catching on fire. It didn't hurt him, and he could fling the fire around like a human flamethrower so long as he stayed pissed off about something. Luckily for Annalisa and the rest of the Neighborhood Watch, there was plenty for him to be mad about at any given time, so they could count on Hothead to provide their firepower, both figuratively and literally. His costume was a red body stocking with decorative orange and yellow puffs at his wrists and ankles that his mom had made to look like fire, even though they were mostly just frizzed-up fabric. He even had a chest logo like a candle flame.

Annalisa and Breezy flew down until they were flanking Hothead as he pedaled up the street toward Wheels' house. His head flames burned bright and hot and Annalisa could see why. Instead of his mountain bike with the big knobby tires, he was riding a pink cruiser with tassels flapping from the handlebars.

"Where's your bike, Cole?" called Breezy.

A jet of flame shot off the top of Hothead's head, narrowly missing Breezy's cape. "I've got a stupid flat tire. Had to borrow my stupid sister's stupid bike."

Breezy wasn't fazed by his near-miss with fiery death. "That's pretty stupid."

"Boys, quit being so stupid." Annalisa felt a twinge of irritation. "We've got a crime to stop."

"Is it a crime? Wheels didn't say." Hothead panted as he pedaled.

Annalisa took pity on him, flew down, and lifted him into the air, bike and all.

Hothead wobbled on his seat. "Whoa, don't drop me! We don't all fly!"

"Don't set me on fire," retorted Annalisa.

The three young heroes crossed over town, heading for the older part where Wheels lived.

Wheels' parents had named her Aighleigh, which was a classy name if difficult for almost anybody to spell. She'd been in a car accident with her parents when she was five. Her dad lived, her mom didn't, and Aighleigh was stuck in a wheelchair, probably for the rest of her life. Somewhere in the process of healing and grieving, her power had surfaced, and it was a rare kind of super-engineering ability, like the supervillain Destroyer had. Aighleigh had used it first to build fantastic and wonderful toys, using cast-off bits of machinery she found around her dad's auto salvage yard. Later, as she grew older, she'd created inventions to help her father run his business, to make their lives easier, and to beef up her wheelchair until it was loaded with more high-tech gizmos and gadgets than anyone might possibly need. Aighleigh had been the first one to want to be a superhero, and she and Annalisa had founded the Neighborhood Watch.

A dozen different satellite dishes and aerials decorated the roof of the Neighborhood Watch headquarters. It had begun life as a Winnebago in the salvage yard, with horrible shag carpet from the Seventies and mice living in the cabinets. Wheels and Annalisa—and later, the others—had worked hard to clean it up and turn it into something of which they could be proud. It might not have been as fancy or high-tech as Just Cause's Fort Justice in New York, but for a handful of twelve-year-olds, it was an impressive improvement. They'd cleaned it, pulled out the carpet and replaced it with tiles salvaged from a trailer wreck. They had old TVs and computer monitors to show off data and images from the tiny cameras Wheels was building and installing all over town with her fleet of drones. There was even a tiny refrigerator that Wheels' dad kept well-stocked with Mexican Coca Cola.

All the kids' parents knew about their children's abilities. For the most part, they were proud of their young would-be superheroes, and so long as the kids didn't get into any real trouble or do anything truly dangerous, it wasn't a problem for them to play at being heroes. If they got themselves into trouble, Annalisa figured she'd be grounded until she was eighteen.

She and Breezy landed outside their HQ, and she carefully set Hothead's bike back on the ground. His temper had subsided enough that only occasional sparks spat from the top of his head. When they'd first started using the Winnebago, they had secret code phrases and knocks and stuff, but now that Wheels had her gear set up around it, nobody could even get close to it without her seeing them coming from a mile away.

Rascal threw open the Winnebago door. "About time you guys got here. We've been waiting for hours." Rascal's real name was Vinnie. Like Hothead, he was wearing his costume. His was a black body stocking with shiny red plastic armor pads on his knees, elbows, chest, and back that were made from melted-down skateboard wheels. The demon-face visor of his helmet was made from the same material. He was a gifted sculptor and artist too, although he chose to turn those talents to tagging just about every surface he could reach throughout town. And with the powers to run up walls and across ceilings, he could reach pretty much any surface. His powers were also great for keeping his feet attached to his skateboard, although at the moment it was stuck to his hip like a gunslinger's pistol.

"We got here as fast as we could," said Breezy.

Rascal looked him up and down. "I mean, is it laundry day?"

Hothead's hair flickered as he grew impatient. "You gonna let us in or what?"

"Oh yeah." Rascal backed out of the door to let the others enter their HQ.

It was cool inside the Winnebago, thanks to the air conditioner Wheels had rigged up on the roof with Annalisa's help. The brains of the Neighborhood Watch was parked amid a nest of TV screens and keyboards. She had her back to the others, instead watching a scene play out on one of the screens before her. "Thanks for coming, you guys."

Annalisa elbowed Breezy, and he grinned back. "Anything to get out of the house on a boring Sunday afternoon."

Wheels tugged on her wheels and turned herself around. She had a smudge of dirt across her chin and her goggles sat up high on her forehead. "Is it laundry day or something?"

"Yes, dang it. My mom said if I didn't let her wash my suit, she was gonna burn it. She said it smelled like a goat." Breezy looked crestfallen.

Annalisa laughed with the others, even though she felt a little bad about it. She hadn't ever noticed

Breezy smelling funky. "Don't worry about it," she said as the giggles subsided. "You got your cape, and that's all you really need for people to know who you are."

"Still, it might be a good idea to have a backup costume," said Wheels. "For laundry day."

More laughter followed, and Annalisa could see Breezy was really starting to get angry about it. She flew up until she was nearly bumping her head against the Winnebago's ceiling. She stuck her fingers in her mouth and blew a sharp whistle loud enough to have hailed a cab on a busy New York City street. It was one of the most useful things her mother had ever taught her how to do.

Everyone quit laughing at Breezy and stuffed their fingers in their ears, a moment too late.

"Dang it, that's loud. My ears are ringing." Hothead glared up at Annalisa.

"That's the idea, Hothead. Now what's this emergency, Wheels?"

Wheels blinked in surprise, clearly having forgotten what it was all about. "Oh. You guys know the Angry Face House up on Park Hill Road?"

Everyone nodded. It was one of the McMansions that sprang up in the lower class neighborhoods during the last economic boom. Annalisa's mom called it *gentrification* but her dad said it was just rich folks trying to crowd out the working class. Angry Face House had oddly-shaped eaves above its windows that made it look like it was glaring at everyone who came up Park Hill Road. It was a local legend, as was the eccentric family who lived in it.

"What about it?" asked Hothead.

"Well, one of the old lady's cats escaped and went up a tree," said Wheels.

"So?" Rascal didn't sound impressed.

"Her grandson climbed up after it. Now he's stuck too."

Annalisa gasped. What a perfect opportunity! "We get to be heroes! *Real* heroes!" She clasped her hands together, feeling like she might burst with excitement.

Breezy nodded. "Looks like."

"That's why I called you," said Wheels. "So, you guys want to go?"

Annalisa nodded. She was first out the door of the Winnebago. "Neighborhood Watch, let's roll!"

Chapter Two

They say getting there is half the fun, and in the Neighborhood Watch, that was no exception. Wheels had a motor in her wheelchair for such journeys, but instead of a pathetic electric motor, she had an engine appropriated from a short-track quarter midget racer. With wide tires for traction and extra outrigger wheels for balance, she could really blaze down the road. She was so fast, in fact, that she had to slow down to keep from outpacing the others. Annalisa was pretty sure someday Wheels would get a speeding ticket, but no police officer would ever believe a twelve-year-old girl had a wheelchair as fast as a patrol car.

Rascal was fearless. He used his powers to stick his feet onto his skateboard and one hand onto Wheels' chair. As her chair howled along, he would hop into the air to clear seams in the pavement, sometimes doing flips just because he could. Annalisa hoped he never fell because he'd leave a trail of red plastic armor and body parts for a quarter mile.

Hothead, of course, couldn't fly, and Wheels didn't have room for a passenger. Breezy's wind wasn't strong enough to carry him either, which left Annalisa. They hadn't yet worked out the best way to carry him. When he tried sitting on her back, her cape flapped in his face, which made him mad, which meant Annalisa's cape would catch fire. He also hated dangling from her arms beneath her, which meant his hair burning right into her face. So far, carrying him on his bike seemed to be the best option. Privately, Annalisa had suggested to Wheels that some kind of trailer or sidecar might be a better option. Wheels promised to look into it, but Annalisa was pretty sure she was dragging her feet on it because she didn't want to have the grouchy superhero riding shotgun.

They raced toward Park Hill Road. People out enjoying the sunny Sunday afternoon whistled and waved as the young heroes passed by. Annalisa tried to smile and wave back to all of them. She knew how important it was for the Neighborhood Watch to keep impressions positive, because the truth of it was they hadn't gotten to do any *real* superhero stuff yet. She and Wheels had discussed it for a long time over a couple of bottles of Mexican Coca Cola in their headquarters on a rainy afternoon when it was just the two of them.

The problem with being superheroes in their sleepy little town was that there wasn't much to keep them busy. Even Just Cause New York, the world's premier superhero team, barely got called into true parapowered action three or four times a year. The rest of the time they were oriented more toward community service. They visited sick kids in hospitals. They helped with rescues or provided security for important events. Rarely did they have the chance to fight supervillains, or to save the world. And if Just Cause didn't see much action, what chance did the Neighborhood Watch have?

Very little, Wheels had said, which was why it was so important for them to be well-liked among the civilians. Especially—and this made Annalisa grind her teeth until it gave her a headache—since they weren't the only game in town.

They called themselves the Culture Club, after some band from Annalisa's mom's youth. There were three of them, all girls. Identical triplets. Each with unique parahuman abilities. Brittany was the leader, and like Annalisa, she was super-strong and could fly. Brianna could move things with her mind. Brooklyn could stretch herself like a rubber band. They didn't even bother with superhero names, instead using their own names like they were brands. They wore matching costumes that seemed to change every other week, thanks to their fashion icon mother and they were always in the news, thanks to their father's position as a local television reporter.

And the worst of it was they all went to the same school as the Neighborhood Watch.

Annalisa was fascinated by the number of parahumans in Malley Middle School's seventh-grade class. She'd memorized enough of the statistics about parahumans to know that her town wasn't large enough to have an average of even one parahuman. Somehow, though, there were eight, and they were all in the same grade at the same school. The odds against such an occurrence were ridiculously low, and someday Annalisa planned to figure out exactly why it had happened. In the meantime, though, she had her team and Brittany had hers, and it seemed like the Neighborhood Watch was always trying to catch up to the Culture Club.

"Come on, you guys, can't you go any faster?" she called to Wheels and Breezy.

Rascal slapped Wheels' back. "Yeah, I ride cars that go faster than this."

Wheels goosed her throttle, but the road was pretty rough and she had to keep steering her chair around potholes. "I'm going as fast as I can risk."

Hothead's hair burned bright. "Come on, we're gonna miss our chance to do *anything*."

"Maybe you and Annalisa—I mean *La Capitána* —should go on ahead," suggested Breezy.

Annalisa wanted to agree with him, but that wouldn't have been right. "No, we're a team. We need to show up together. Maybe we won't . . ."

She didn't finish her sentence, not wanting to put it out there that they might be too late.

But of course, they were.

As they approached the Angry Face House, Annalisa's heart sank. She saw the KTVG news van amid the flashing lights of police cars and fire trucks. Of course it was there, because the Culture Club was there. Brittany already had the errant grandson gathered in her arms as was gently floating down from the upper branches. Brianna had used her mind powers to pull the cat away from the tree where Brooklyn could stretch her arms up to gather it in. She retrieved the cat as Brittany touched down to the ground with the boy. He giggled as she solemnly took her fashionable silk scarf off and draped it around his neck with a smile and gentle admonishment to behave himself.

The Neighborhood Watch came to a screeching halt well outside the circle of attention and admiration commanded by the Culture Club. A few people glanced back at the newcomers but mostly they kept their attention on the identical triplets as they addressed the crowd.

"Hi, everyone, and thanks for coming out to support us today!" said Brittany as the crowd applauded. "Remember, the Culture Club isn't just me and my sisters. It's all of you, too." The applause transformed into cheers. The triplets basked in it. They all wore tight black jeans with midriff-exposing white button-down shirts and multicolored silk scarves. Annalisa grimaced, knowing that half the girls in school Monday would be dressed the same way. So much for her simple star-logo t-shirt.

"That's so rehearsed," grumbled Wheels as Annalisa landed beside her. "I bet her parents make her memorize that."

"Do you see their dad?" asked Hothead. "Or is that just a regular news van?"

"I don't see him," said Breezy. "Maybe he's inside it?"

"More likely they're so famous now they don't need him to talk them up every time they show up." Hothead's hair flashed into bright flames and he crossed his arms. "It's not fair."

"What's not fair?" asked Rascal, pirouetting on his rear wheels.

"Every time we have a chance to do something, to be real superheroes, they get there first."

Annalisa stepped back from the heat pouring off Hothead. "Yeah, it sucks."

"Hothead . . ." Wheels sounded urgent.

"It sucks? It *sucks*? We're missing every chance and all you can say is it *sucks*?" A glob of flame shot into the sky.

"Hothead!" Wheels yelled.

He turned around to face her. "What?"

"You're melting your sister's bike."

Everyone turned to see the pink bicycle sagging under Hothead's heat. The tires were bubbling like chili on the stove.

"Is there a problem over here?" A fireman trotted over, an extinguisher at the ready.

Annalisa interposed herself between him and Hothead, floating up so she'd be at eye level and maybe would carry a little more authority than if she stayed on the ground to look up at him. "It's fine. We just came to, uh, to make sure there wasn't more than the Culture Club could handle."

The fireman's eyes widened. "Oh, now I recognize you. You're those junior superheroes. The New Kids on the Block or something."

"The Neighborhood Watch," said Wheels.

"Sure, whatever you like. Listen, we can't have you guys out here spraying fire around like, uh, Matchstick here."

"Hothead," said Breezy.

The fireman looked at him. "Is that your costume?"

Breezy grimaced.

"'Bye, everyone!" called Brittany from the circle of adoring fans. She flew into the sky with her arms around her sisters. Brianna used her powers to help her sister fly with the extra weight while Brooklyn stretched an arm around all of them like a seat belt. They headed off toward the wealthy part of town.

The fireman watched them go and then turned back to Annalisa. "You kids had better go, and tell Firehair there behind you to get himself under control or I'm going to have to douse him with this." He held up the extinguisher so everyone could see it.

"All right, all right. Jeez." Hothead kicked at the ground in disgust.

Annalisa saw he was making a real effort to calm down and get his fire under control and looked at the fireman. "You sure everything is okay over there? If there's any trouble, or anyone needs help, well, that's why we're here."

"I'm sure everything is getting along just fine without you," said the Fireman. Rascal wandered around behind him, uncapping a Sharpie as he went.

Annalisa's eyes grew wide. Getting busted was the last thing any of them needed. "Uh, well, we're here to help. It took us longer to, uh, to get here than we thought because . . . because . . ."

"Because we were busy being superheroes," said Wheels, coming to the rescue. "That's what we do."

"Yeah, son," said Breezy. "That's what we do."

Rascal came around from behind the fireman and Annalisa stopped holding her breath in relief. "Look, kids, this town already has a superhero team, and they're called the Culture Club. I'd be more worried about the five of you getting hurt trying to do something you're not prepared for."

"What do you mean, *not prepared*?" asked Annalisa. "We're prepared. We've got powers. We practice and stuff."

"You're just kids, and parahuman powers aren't as uncommon as they used to be when I was your age. You might have abilities, but that doesn't make you superheroes any more than carrying a fire extinguisher makes you a fireman." He raised a finger, assuming the lecturing position that so many adults took when they were telling kids what they could and couldn't do.

Annalisa hated that pose. "Okay, fine, we're leaving. There's nothing left for us to do here, anyway."

The fireman nodded. "Good." He turned to leave and Annalisa saw that Rascal had somehow managed to write *KICK ME* on the man's back in permanent marker. She stifled a laugh, as did the rest of her team.

"All right, guys, let's go back to HQ. We need to figure out what to do next," Annalisa said.

Wheels frowned. "There's not much for us to do except watch the news coverage."

"It's not fair," said Hothead. "They're not any better than us. Why do they always get all the attention?"

"Because they get to things first," said Breezy.

"But how do they do that? Don't they get the same alerts we get?"

Breezy shrugged. "Maybe it doesn't take them as long to get going as we do."

"Maybe if you had your costume, we could go faster." Hothead's hair flashed again.

"Stop it, Cole. That's not helping anything," said Annalisa. "It's not about costumes. It's about being in the right place at the right time. We just need to be better at that than they are."

"We need to be better at *everything* than they are so people like that fireman will take us seriously," said Rascal.

"Writing insults isn't going to get anyone taken seriously," said Wheels.

"But it sure felt good." Rascal chuckled and the others laughed with him.

They turned to head back toward their headquarters, this time at a much more leisurely rate. There was no need to hurry now that the emergency had ended and they had once again arrived too late to do anything. Hothead hung his head, not even radiating the slightest bit of heat, as he contemplated how he would explain that he'd melted his sister's bike. Annalisa felt bad for him, but then, she felt bad for all of them. How were they ever going to become *real* superheroes if they couldn't even manage a simple task of getting a cat out of a tree?

The answer was as simple as any could be: they had to be better than the Culture Club.

Annalisa just had to figure out how.

Chapter Three

Annalisa got out the door so late the next morning she had to fly to catch the school bus. She hated that she had to do it at all. She didn't understand why her mom was so insistent upon her riding the stupid bus when she could fly. Flying was even safer, she argued, because she was less likely to get into a traffic accident or be bullied or anything like that. It didn't matter. Her mother was as powerful as a supervillain when it came to laying down the law. The law in this case was Annalisa would ride the school bus like a normal child.

She hated using her powers when she wasn't in her costume. It wasn't like she had to protect her identity or anything—her costume didn't even have a mask. But when she was just being plain old Annalisa Torres instead of La Capitána, she felt like using her powers was *cheating*. Normal kids couldn't do what she did, and she didn't want to show off in front of them. But when she had to ride the stupid school bus and was late to the stop, she had to fly after it.

A few kids pressed their noses against the bus windows as she flew past, because staring at a parahuman never grew old. The rest didn't bother to look up from their phones, like a bunch of technozombies. Annalisa passed the front of the bus and waved at the driver, hoping Mac would take pity and stop. *Mac* was short for Ms. Macready, who was the perpetually grumpy driver with the frizzy gray ponytail, ball cap, and reek of cheap cigarettes. None of the kids liked her and it was plain the feeling was mutual. Annalisa wouldn't have been surprised if she had to follow the bus all the way to the next stop before Mac would let her on board, but the bus signaled and swung over to the curb.

"Thanks, Mac!" Annalisa climbed the steps, pretending she was like every other kid who couldn't fly.

Mac grunted something unintelligible and pointed her thumb towards the back of the bus.

Annalisa spotted a familiar head of short dreadlocks and hurried back to sit in the vacant spot beside him before Mac launched the bus toward its next destination. "Hey, Breezy." He was the only other kid in the Neighborhood Watch who rode the school bus. Wheels had her own short bus thanks to her wheelchair, and Hothead and Rascal lived close enough to the school not to need a bus at all.

Breezy looked up from his phone, pulled his earbuds out, and grinned at her. "Hey, Cap." He opened the top of his backpack to show off costume, neatly folded and compressed into a plastic zip-top bag. "Just in case, you know?"

"Yeah, I know." Annalisa set her backpack in her lap. In superhero movies, the heroes wore their costumes underneath their clothes. She'd tried it once only to discover it was both impractical and uncomfortable. She kept her cape rolled up in a separate pocket of her backpack in the unlikely event she'd ever need to be a superhero during school hours. She figured the cape was all the costume she would ever really need. "You expecting trouble today?"

Breezy cleared his throat and dropped his voice into as low a register it would go, which wasn't very because his voice hadn't changed yet. "I'm *always* expecting trouble."

Annalisa snickered. Quite honestly, she'd love to find some kind of trouble requiring superheroic intervention. The main problem with living in such a sleepy town was never finding a convenient supervillain around when you really needed one. The rest of the bus ride, she worked on math homework she hadn't gotten around to completing over the weekend while Breezy slipped his earbuds back in and closed his eyes.

At last, the bus pulled into the school's circle drive and Mac opened the doors. The kids filed out, blinking in the bright spring sunshine, staggering under the actual weight of their backpacks and the metaphysical weight of their middle-school lives. "See you after school, Breezy."

Breezy nodded. "Yeah, later." He was in a different pod than she was, so their paths never crossed during the school day except during all-school assemblies and the like. Annalisa kind of wished they had classes together. She'd never admit it to anyone, but there was something about the dark-skinned boy's smile she really liked.

First bell rang and the kids hit the halls like waves breaking against the shore. Annalisa hurried to her locker and threw her backpack inside. Her math pages were crumpled but she had managed to finish them all. She knew the Hero Academy would take most parahumans as students, but if she had good grades, it would put her on the best track possible to get into Just Cause someday. Sometimes she even ate lunch in the library so she could make sure she had enough time to get all her work done. The more she did during school hours meant more time for superheroics afterward, or at least surfing the internet for parahuman videos and news.

She slipped into her seat in first period, Sustained Silent Reading. A lot of kids brought in comic books or magazines. Unlike them, Annalisa was working her way through Dr. Matasuko Musashi's *The Origin of Parapowers*, which would have been dense reading for a college student, never mind a twelve-year old. More than once, her teacher had gently suggested perhaps she might try reading something a little more appropriate for her age level, but Annalisa wouldn't be deterred. She was on her third time reading through the book, and each time it felt like she learned a little more about parahumans.

"Good morning, Malley students. These are your announcements." The school receptionist sounded bored as her voice came over the classroom's speaker. Annalisa ignored the announcements until the receptionist said, "There will be an assembly after sixth period to honor Malley Middle School's own superheroes, the Culture Club. All students will attend."

Annalisa looked up at the speaker box and glared. If she had heat vision or laser eyes or something, it wouldn't have stood a chance. She glanced across the classroom at Cole, who was squeezing his hands into fists to try to keep his head from bursting into flame. She knew exactly how he felt. He saw her looking his way and she shook her head slightly so he'd know she agreed with him. His eyes softened a bit and and she knew they were past the worst of it. Using his power in school, even accidentally, was a guaranteed suspension and possible expulsion. It was one thing the administrators had made very clear to all the kids who had known abilities. So far, they'd all managed to keep out of trouble, but Annalisa suspected it was only a matter of time before one of them slipped up somehow and then there would be severe consequences.

She kept her head down the rest of the morning, burying herself in her schoolwork to keep her mind off the upcoming assembly. The temptation to ditch was strong, but she had to be better than that. At least with it being a school-wide assembly, she'd be able to sit with her only real friends in the Neighborhood Watch. They didn't have to applaud. They didn't have to support the bullies of the Culture Club.

And bullies is what they were, for it seemed like every day Brittany, Brianna, and Brooklyn found some way to get in a snide remark, or a shove, or some perfectly-timed hidden use of their powers to hurt or hinder someone. To many of the students in the school, they were the popular trend-setters, to be admired and accoladed. Annalisa, on the other hand, could quite cheerfully have dumped each of them in the lunchroom trash cans if she could have gotten away with it. Especially as many times as they'd been on her case. She knew it was because she had powers like they did, as did her friends. The Neighborhood Watch was a favorite target for the bullying antics of the Culture Club, and because the triplets were *so* heroic, *so* locally famous, they could do no wrong.

Brittany could shove Annalisa into a locker hard enough to dent it, in full view of a teacher, and somehow it would be Annalisa's fault. It had happened before; it would probably happen again.

The bell rang and Annalisa went to her locker to collect her lunch. She figured she would eat in the library. Maybe Torvald, the librarian, would have some good recommendation for another book about parahumans for her to read—

A hard hip struck her perfectly in her ribs, knocking her off-balance and crushing her lunch in between Annalisa and her locker. Brittany looked back over her shoulder. "Oh, sorry. I didn't see you there, *Anal*-eesa. You're so little." Brianna and Brooklyn laughed like it was the funniest thing they'd ever heard. Several of the other kids in the hallway likewise broke into giggles, because laughing at the Culture Club's jokes was one of the best ways to be part of the In Crowd.

Annalisa turned away from the Culture Club as they continued down the hall toward the lunchroom. She was *definitely* going to the library, and only there because she couldn't get any further away from the triplets without leaving campus altogether, which was strictly forbidden. The school couldn't do much to her if she left, but her mom would ground her until she was thirty.

Torvald the librarian was a lanky, slender young man with thick black-rimmed glasses, perpetually-tousled blonde hair, and scraggly whiskers decorating his chin. He preferred tea to coffee, swords-and-sorcery fantasy to space opera, and Wagner to Vivaldi. He was also the closest thing Annalisa had to a true grown-up friend. She'd salvaged what she could from her smashed lunch—a peanut butter sandwich, some potato chip crumbs, and some carrot sticks—and drifted up the stairs to the library, not caring if someone saw her flying or not. She strolled into the library, taking in the warm smell of books and felt the stress melting away. Torvald sat behind the desk, scanning in the bar codes on books that students had returned.

"Hi, Torvald. Can I eat in here today?"

Torvald looked up from his work and smiled at her. "Of course, Annalisa. Oh! I have something for you." He set a hardcover book atop the counter.

Annalisa picked it up and looked at the cover. *On Parahuman Combat, Third Edition* by Estella Echevarrìa. She knew that name. Echevarrìa was the principal of the Hero Academy, and before that, she'd been the Just Cause hero known as Sunstorm. Her heart skipped a beat as she ran a hand down the spine.

"Open it up," said Torvald.

Annalisa opened the cover and saw handwriting on the first page. *Study hard! Good luck!* And then there was a scribble that looked suspiciously like a signature.

"This is an actual textbook used at the Hero Academy." Torvald's grin ran from ear to ear. "There's a newer edition out this year, so this one wound up in the Academy's library. I managed to pull a few strings and get hold of this copy on an interlibrary loan. I figured you might like a break from reading Dr. Musashi's book." He lowered his voice. "I have it on good authority that this particular textbook may have belonged to Mustang Sally at some point."

Annalisa felt like her entire body might burst at such incredible news. Mustang Sally was her favorite hero. Even though Annalisa had a completely different power set, it still meant she was holding a book that had once belonged to the woman in charge of Just Cause New York. It almost made her dizzy to feel like she was so close to such a powerful and influential person. "Th-thank you." She realized she was close to tears.

Torvald smiled. "Take good care of it. That's a one of a kind book. It's meant for a higher reading level than middle schoolers, but I know you're a strong reader and I think you'll learn a lot from it."

Annalisa felt so good about the new book she didn't even realize she was floating until she turned to go sit down and discovered her feet weren't on the floor. Torvald winked at her and she knew she wouldn't be in trouble for it. She sat at a study table, unpacked what of her lunch had survived the collision with Brianna, and opened the book to the first page.

It was definitely a text meant for higher readers, but Annalisa worked her way through the introduction. She was so engrossed in the book she didn't notice the warning bell until Torvald came over and knocked gently on the table beside her. She gasped and looked up in surprise.

"Better put it away for now," said the librarian. "I don't want you to be late to your next class."

Annalisa looked at her phone, realized what time it was, and jammed the book into her backpack. She looked down at her half-eaten, half-ruined lunch. "Torvald, I . . ."

He smiled. "I'll take care of it, Annalisa. Have a great afternoon, okay?"

"Okay!" She ran from the library, remembering to keep her feet on the ground, keeping her pace just slow enough not to attract attention of any hall monitors. She made it into her seat in Social Studies just as the second bell finished. All she had to do was survive the rest of the afternoon, get through the stupid assembly, and then she could go home and spend all evening paging through her new book.

It was a good plan, but the Culture Club had other ideas.

Chapter Four

Brooklyn started it, and her sisters joined in with all the gleeful cruelty of kids frying ants with a magnifying glass.

Annalisa only had to survive two classes until the assembly, and then after that she could go home and really dive into *On Parahuman Combat*. Social Studies wasn't her best subject, but she didn't hate it. At least they touched on bits of parahumans throughout history from time to time. After that was Language Arts, which wouldn't be so bad except that the Culture Club was in it.

They always sat in the very back of the class, goofing on their phones and whispering back and forth. They rarely bothered to pay attention to Mrs. Terminello at all. Why should they? They were so well-loved, they were getting an assembly dedicated to them.

Annalisa sat as far away from them as she could without sitting in the very front of the class. Only dorks sat there, and she'd rather just be invisible. She was already a dork in the eyes of the triplets. She tried to pay attention to Mrs. Terminello, but every suppressed giggle, every sarcastic snort, every whispered remark was like a car alarm going off right behind her. Still, she kept her calm, kept her cool. Faced forward, like she was supposed to do. Heroes triumphed in the face of adversity, she thought.

And then a sharp finger flicked her expertly in the ear, and she yelped in surprise. The class laughed, and nobody did harder than the Culture Club, who was sitting some five seats behind her.

Mrs. Terminello cleared her throat. "Annalisa, is there something you'd like to share with the class?"

Annalisa wanted to say yes, but all that would do was get her flagged as a tattletale by the rest of the class, and that would make the bullying worse all around. "No," she mumbled.

Mrs. Terminello fixed her gaze on Annalisa for a moment before continuing with her lecture. "Now as I was saying, the predicate . . ."

Annalisa didn't care about predicates. Instead, she made a surreptitious glance behind her. Nobody was in the seat immediately behind her. The boy two seats back was fat and probably couldn't have sneaked up behind her without her noticing. But Brooklyn was leaning against her desk in such a way

34

as to hide her arms. Annalisa suspected she was stretching a hand forward along the floor, snaking it between the desk and chair feet, until she reached up right behind Annalisa's head to flick her ear. The second time it happened, Annalisa was ready. She jumped to her feet, whirled around, and grabbed hold of Brooklyn's hand to show Mrs. Terminello that she wasn't at fault.

At least, that's what *should* have happened.

What *actually* happened was that when Annalisa started to jump up, something heavy tugged at the back of her pants. It pulled her off balance and she came down on the edge of her chair instead of back into it. The chair legs slipped on the threadbare carpet and dumped her on her side in the aisle where she discovered someone had padlocked her backpack to her belt loop without her noticing it.

"Annalisa!" shouted Mrs. Terminello.

"It's not my fault!" cried Annalisa. "Look!" She twisted to show off her predicament, but by that time, of course, the Culture Club had removed the padlock.

Mrs. Terminello sighed. "I think you'd better explain yourself to the office." She picked up her desk phone and waited until the school receptionist at the other end answered. "Egret? I'm sending a student down there for misbehavior. Yes, that's right. Annalisa Torres." She hung up and turned back to Annalisa. "Egret is expecting you. Detention the rest of the day."

Annalisa's sigh parroted Mrs. Terminello's as she picked up her backpack and slung it over one shoulder with all the weariness of Atlas bearing the weight of the world on his shoulders. As she trudged out of the class, she saw Brianna flashing the padlock at her where Mrs. Terminello couldn't see it but Annalisa could. Brianna's grin was the most evil, twisted thing she had ever seen.

She walked slowly through the halls, in no hurry to make it to the office. It wasn't the first time she'd served an in-school detention. It probably wouldn't be the last, she thought. At least they'd let her read, she thought, which made it seem better. And maybe, if she was lucky, they wouldn't let her attend the assembly. That thought brightened her up enough that she was almost grinning as she sauntered into the office.

"In trouble again, Annalisa?" asked Egret. The school receptionist had blonde dreadlocks and always wore a fresh flower in her hair.

Annalisa nodded.

Egret motioned to the study desk along one wall of the office. "Go ahead and have a seat. You can work on homework or read quietly, but no phone and no earbuds."

Annalisa cleared her throat. "Uh, what about the assembly? Do I have to stay here or go to it?"

Egret gave her a knowing smile. "I'm afraid you'll have to miss it, unless you'd rather serve that part of your in-school detention tomorrow morning."

"No, I'll do it now." Annalisa turned away from Egret so the woman wouldn't see her wide smile. She sat at the table and quickly became fully-absorbed in the text of *On Parahuman Combat*. She'd never thought so much about how her powers would be useful for fighting, but that she might even *have* to fight was a bit of a new concept for her. She supposed it was part of the job, being a superhero. She would fight lots of battles over her career, and with super-strength and flight, she'd be an important part of any battle. At twelve, she hadn't given much thought to what she would do if she ever had to fight another parahuman. As the days went by, the idea of a big knock-down drag-out with the Culture Club not only seemed inevitable, but something she welcomed. She longed to punch Brianna right in her stupid face.

The sound of cheering and someone shouting through a microphone filtered into the office and Annalisa knew the assembly was in full swing. The Culture Club was getting their accolades. At least she didn't have to watch as the Malley students bent their knees and swore their undying allegiance to the triplets. She did wonder what her fellow Neighborhood Watch partners thought about it. She'd have to ask them later.

Egret touched her shoulder and Annalisa jumped. "Didn't you hear me? You're done, Annalisa. School's out. You can go home now."

Annalisa looked down at the book. She'd gotten through the first two chapters and her mind was whirling with all kinds of new possibilities. She longed to meet a *real* supervillain so she could try out some of the things she'd learned. "Do you know about any supervillains around here?" She asked Egret as she slung her backpack over her shoulder.

"I don't, Annalisa, and that's a good thing. I remember when the Archmage fought Just Cause. I was your age at the time. It was a very scary thing to see on the news. The farther we are from supervillains, the better we all are."

Annalisa wanted to ask Egret more about the Archmage. She'd read some articles online about that event, but hadn't ever met anyone who knew anything about it. She could tell it bothered Egret though. "Don't worry, Egret. If any supervillains come around, we'll take care if them."

"The Neighborhood Watch?" Egret smiled.

Annalisa gasped. "You know about us?"

"Of course I do. It's my job to know about Malley students."

"Do you . . . think we have a chance?"

"A chance at what? To be superheroes?"

Annalisa nodded.

Egret patted Annalisa's shoulder. "I think you can be anything you want to be, Annalisa, including a superhero. Now get out of here. I have work to do before I leave."

"Thanks, Egret!" Annalisa adjusted her backpack straps and left the office, feeling much better about herself. Even seeing the bus pull away from the school without her on it didn't dampen her spirits. She texted her mom. *Can I go to the library?* The library was only a few blocks away and she was allowed to walk over there on her own. She could hang out there for a couple of hours and then her mom could pick her up there after her shift was done at the doctor's office where she worked.

Her mom replied with an affirmative so Annalisa headed out into the warm spring afternoon, enjoying the sunlight on her skin. She texted Wheels as she walked. *How was the assembly?*

Stupid, came Wheels' reply. *Where were you?*

Detention.

Lucky.

IKR?

A blaring horn made Annalisa jump. She looked up to see a truck trying to leave a construction site and the driver motioning at her to get out of the way. She hurried across the entrance and watched as the truck pulled away. It was an armored truck with a bank logo on the side, and she didn't think anything about it until she heard a low moan nearby. The sound startled her even more than the truck's horn had. Her first instinct was to run away from whatever had made the noise, but she was curious, and she was feeling like a superhero, and superheroes didn't run away like a scaredy-cat.

She slipped around the edge of the fence around the job site. Nobody was working there.

She didn't know why. Maybe they'd all gone home. But why had there been a bank truck there? The moaning sound repeated and she realized it was coming from inside the big blue dumpster. It was too tall for her to see inside. She glanced around but nobody else was around. She flew up to peek over the edge of the dumpster, excited and terrified at what she might find.

There, lying on a pile of construction trash, were two men stripped down to their underwear. They were trussed up with duct tape, binding their wrists and ankles together. More duct tape was wrapped around their heads to seal their mouths. One looked like he was asleep, or more likely unconscious, given the way one of his eyes was swollen shut. The other man was sort of awake. He looked like he'd been punched too, but his undamaged eye was rolling like he was barely awake. Annalisa made a surprised squeak when she saw them and the man who was conscious looked her way. He yelled for help—at least, Annalisa thought he did, although the duct tape muffled him.

Annalisa struggled past her fear and flew over the edge of the dumpster to land beside the men. "Are you okay?" She realized as soon as she asked that the man had no way to answer her, nor to answer any of the other questions she had, like why they were in the dumpster, why they didn't have any clothes, and who had tied them up.

The man seemed frantic. He kept repeating the same two words through his duct tape gag. She couldn't understand him and realized she didn't have any way to cut the tape. "Hang on, I'm going to go find a tool to cut the tape."

She flew out of the dumpster, gritting her teeth against the man's frantic, muffled cries. She figured one of the big trucks or forklifts parked around the site would have something sharp she could use, and after a minute of searching, she found a pair of shears. She brought them back to the man and he stopped his bellowing when she held them up for him to see.

"I'll be careful, I promise." She started working the shears through the tape, just in front of his ear so she wouldn't accidentally cut it. The tape was slick with the man's sweat and she was grossed out just by touching it, but she was a *superhero* and she couldn't let such a minor inconvenience dissuade her from doing the right thing. After a few seconds of careful work, the tape parted and she pulled it away from the man's mouth.

"Call the police," he said right away. "That guy stole the armored truck!"

"What guy?" Annalisa pulled out her phone.

"The . . . the guy. I don't know who he was. At first he looked like Ray. Ray's our third. The guy who rides in the back. But then he caught us by surprise. Knocked us out. When he left, he looked like me."

"He changed his face?" Annalisa's thumb froze halfway through punching 9-1-1 onto her phone. "Like he has parapowers?"

"Yes. No. I don't know. Look, kid, are you going to call the police or what? If not, cut me loose and let me use your phone."

"A supervillain . . ." Annalisa looked in the direction the armored truck had turned. It was only a few minutes. It couldn't have gone that far. Besides, she could find it a lot easier than most people, thanks to her bird's-eye view.

"Kid . . . come on!"

Annalisa finished dialing. The operator came on almost immediately. "9-1-1, what's your emergency?"

"This is . . ." Annalisa stopped, suddenly terrified. What was she supposed to say? She'd never made an emergency call before. "I'm calling to report a stolen armored truck and two, uh, guards tied up and left in a dumpster."

"Who is this?" The dispatcher sounded suspicious. Annalisa couldn't blame her. Given the same circumstances, she'd be suspicious too.

"This is La Capitána, of the Neighborhood Watch. I'm a—a superhero. You need to send the police to the construction site near Malley Middle School. There's two guys tied up in a dumpster and they need help. I'm going to go after the stolen truck."

"You're what? No, don't do that. You stay where you are, miss. Are you there now?"

Annalisa floated out of the dumpster, much to the chagrin of the man still taped up in it. "Hey! Hey kid, come back! Come on, cut me loose!" he yelled.

"Miss? What's going on? Miss?" The dispatched called into the phone.

"Sorry, I have to go. Please come help these guys." Annalisa hung up. She looked down at the men in the dumpster. "I'm sorry. Help is on the way. I'm going to go get your truck back." She fumbled in her backpack and found her cape. She hung her backpack up on a nearby light pole where she could find it again but nobody would take it. Then she tied the cape around her neck. "Don't worry, I'm a superhero."

"Kid! Hey! Come back!"

Annalisa almost turned around. She felt terribly guilty about leaving the man tied up behind her, but she kind of thought if she'd cut him free, he'd try to stop her from stopping a real live supervillain. Maybe he'd think he was protecting her, but she didn't need protecting. She'd capture the supervillain and take him to the police herself. Then maybe the school would have an assembly for her. Oh, and her teammates, too. She couldn't do all the superheroing and leave nothing for them. That's the kind of thing the Culture Club would do, but she was a better person than that.

She opened the Neighborhood Watch app. "Now hear this . . ." she said into the phone, which would record her message and send it to the other

Neighborhood Watch heroes. "This is La Capitána. A real supervillain just stole an armored truck. He tied up two guards and left them in a dumpster. I'm looking for the truck now. Get ready to head out because I'll need backup for sure." She finished her message, keyed *send*, and nodded. That would have to do.

The troops had been called out. All that remained was for her to find the stolen armored truck. With her cape flapping majestically in her wake, La Capitána went off to save the day.

Chapter Five

Red, Annalisa decided. The armored truck had definitely been red. It had six wheels and a real jerk behind the wheel. She wondered where it was going. Cutting through the tape holding the man in the dumpster had taken a few minutes, and even though it was rush hour, the truck could have gone quite a way.

"Hey, Wheels?" Annalisa used the chat function of the Neighborhood Watch app to connect directly with her teammate.

"What's up, Capitána? And you said there's a supervillain? A real one?"

"Yeah. He's a real douche bag. He almost ran me over, and he duct taped a couple of guards and threw them into a dumpster."

"Wow, that's . . . I mean, I can't believe it. A real supervillain after all this time! We must have finally earned our good karma."

"Well I don't know about that, but can you get into local security cameras? I need help looking for this stolen armored truck."

Somebody shouted something that Wheels' speaker couldn't quite pick up.

"What's that?" asked Annalisa.

"That's, uh, Rascal. He says he's got an idea." Her voice grew faint as she turned away from her phone. "Use your phone, stupid. that's why you have it."

A picture of Rascal popped up on Annalisa's phone. She only sort of paid attention to it. Most of her focus was working on finding the missing truck. How hard could it be to find a red truck? Of course, it would help if she knew which direction it had gone after nearly running her over. She should have paid more attention.

" . . . she saw it," said Rascal.

"Wait, what? Say that again. I, uh, I was looking for that truck."

"I said, I put it out on Twitter and one of my followers said she saw it."

"You're on Twitter?"

"I mean . . . yeah. *At TeamRascal.* I tweet how awesome I am and how awesome we are and I've got like two hundred followers. Most of them are here in town. They're kind of like my live cameras, you know?"

Annalisa actually stopped flying and hovered in midair, astonished at how smart of an idea it was. Why hadn't she thought of that? Or Wheels?

Then she realized, that was why she was part of a team. She couldn't think of everything all the time. None of them could. But if one of them had a great idea, it was a benefit to them all. That's why they had a headquarters, and an app, and now they had a network of spies too. She grinned. The Culture Club wouldn't stand a chance. "Where did she say she saw the truck?"

Rascal told her.

It took Annalisa a minute to get her bearings. Everything looked different when flying over the city. Luckily, she had her GPS app to keep her oriented. She spotted the area where Rascal's follower had reported the missing truck and there it was: a big red truck with a white roof, parked in front of . . . a *bank*.

"No way," she said. "Is he gonna rob a bank?"

She wondered what she should do. As far as she knew, there was only one guy, and she didn't see him in the truck, which meant he was probably know the building already. She knew from TV that guards had to take money between the bank and armored truck. But this guy wasn't a real guard. He was going to just walk out with all the money and nobody would know.

Annalisa would have to stop him. She couldn't wait for the others. She hoped they were hurrying her way, but they weren't firemen sleeping in their clothes. It took time for a bunch of twelve-year-olds to get anywhere individually, much less as a group.

"Oh God, what are *you* doing here? You're not supposed to be here!"

The unexpected voice made Annalisa whirl around in midair. Brittany of the Culture Club was floating ten feet away. She looked as fashionable as ever and thoroughly disgusted to see Annalisa. "It's, uh . . ." Annalisa didn't want to tell Brittany, to give away the one possibility of being a real superhero for once in her life, but she was scared. "A guy stole that truck down there. I think he's robbing the bank."

Brittany seemed unimpressed. "So? What are you going to do, stop it?"

Annalisa turned in midair and put her hands on her hips. She hoped she looked heroic. "Yeah, I am."

Brittany snorted. "You and what army? I don't see the rest of your stupid friends."

"They're not stupid, and they'll be here." An idea occurred to Annalisa. "What are *you* doing here? And where are your stupid sisters?"

Brittany sniffed. "Original much? I don't have to answer to you, Captain Crunch."

Annalisa's cheeks grew hot. "That's La Capitána to you, and you better not forget it."

Brittany flew closer. Annalisa clenched her fists. Were they going to have it out right there, floating over the city? She was ready, but she couldn't remember anything she'd read in Sunstorm's book. She'd barely gotten through the first chapter. Still, she wouldn't back down. Not to the likes of Brittany, even with her getting all up in Annalisa's face. "You know what you are?"

Annalisa didn't get the chance to find out what Brittany thought she was, for at that moment the bank doors burst open and a man in guard attire rushed out, bearing a large duffel bag. She gaped in astonishment as he whirled and fired a pistol back toward the bank doors. "It's really a robbery!" Her first thought was she should call the police, but then she felt the tug of her cape around her neck and she knew.

This was her chance.

People on the street below screamed as the man fired his pistol again. They ducked behind parked cars or into nearby buildings. The man threw the duffel bag into the front seat of the armored truck and ran around to the driver's side. Annalisa didn't know if she was bulletproof, but this was no time to find out. She glared at Brittany and flew down to the back of the truck. Once there, she grabbed hold of the bumper, digging into the tough steel with her super-strength, and lifted.

The truck was much heavier than she expected, and she barely got it an inch off the ground. She knew she couldn't hold it by herself. Not and keep it from driving away. She looked up to see Brittany staring down at her open-mouthed. "Help me!"

Brittany snapped into action. "Come on, Culture Club!" Her shout brought Brianna and Brooklyn out of a nearby coffee shop. They skidded to a halt when they saw Annalisa struggling to hold the armored truck off the road. "Just run with it," said Brittany. She landed beside Annalisa and added her own strength to lifting. The truck's rear wheels came up just as the driver hit the accelerator. The engine revved and the wheels spun, but between Annalisa and Brittany, the truck didn't go anywhere.

Brianna used her mind powers to drag two jack stands from a nearby auto parts store. She slid them beneath the truck's axle, holding taking the weight away from Annalisa and Brittany.

Brittany immediately flew around to the driver's side and wrenched the door open. The driver staggered out, disoriented, with blue paint dripping off his face. He had his gun out but before he could point it at anyone, Brooklyn stretched her arm around from the safety of the far side if the truck and disarmed the man.

Annalisa saw her opportunity. She flew past Brittany, squeezed her eyes shut, and punched the man in the jaw the way she'd once hit a training dummy Wheels had made for her. The dummy had only taken the one punch and fallen apart. The would-be bank robber also only took one punch, and when Annalisa cracked open her eyes, he was lying knocked out on the pavement and her knuckles were smeared with blue.

"Whoa!" cried one of the braver onlookers. "Look, the Culture Club has a new member!"

More people started shouting, and cheering, and applauding. Brooklyn and Brianna ran over to Brittany, who was still holding the armored truck door. "What do we do?"

Brittany looked at the onlookers, then over at Annalisa. "This." She flew over to Annalisa. Then she grabbed Annalisa's dye-smeared hand and raised it above her head. "Our newest member!"

Annalisa gasped. Of all the things that might have happened, it was the most unexpected. And yet, people were cheering and clapping, not just for the Culture Club, but for her.

It felt really, really good.

Chapter Six

"Mamá, Papi, guess what?" Annalisa burst into the house, so excited she couldn't keep her feet on the ground. She kept drifting upward until she realized she was about to bump her head on the ceiling. "I—"

"Annalisa? Come into the kitchen, please."

Annalisa dropped her bag by the door. She'd almost forgotten to go back and get it at the construction site after she'd left the bank. It was no wonder. After all, she'd gotten her hand shaken by the bank manager, the police officers who took the would-be robber into custody, and even gotten grudging approval from the Culture Club. She might have stayed even longer to talk to the press if a small voice in the back of her mind hadn't bugged her about getting home before dinner or she'd be grounded. She was almost home when she remembered her bag and had to fly back to go get it. It had been where she left it, but the two men who'd been taped up in the dumpster were long gone.

Something about the tone of her mom's voice dampened Annalisa's enthusiasm as effectively as dunking a match in a glass of water. She poked her head into the kitchen and saw her mom had tomato soup in a pot on the stove and was layering three different kinds of slices to make grilled cheese sandwiches since it was her turn to cook. Her dad sat at the kitchen table already, working on a beer after a long day of pouring cement. Annalisa kind of liked it when it was her dad's turn to handle dinner, because sometimes he would bring home pizza or fried chicken. Her mom always cooked, even if it was something as simple as soup and grilled cheese. She worked in the HR department for some kind of financial company downtown. "Mamá?"

"Annalisa, I got an email from your school today about your in-school suspension. Would you like to tell me what happened?" Her mom commenced buttering pieces of bread.

Annalisa glanced at her dad. His heavy brows wound together in a frown but he said nothing. She wouldn't get any help from him. Not for something like this. "It's not my fault—"

"Stop," said her mom. "Annalisa, I didn't ask whose fault it was. I asked what happened."

Annalisa looked down at her shoes, firmly planted on the floor instead of floating above it. "There were some, uh, some girls. They were kind of . . . teasing me."

"And?"

"And I told them to stop."

"*Halcónita*, you didn't use your powers on them, did you?" *Halcónita* was her father's nickname for her. It meant *little falcon*. He was very proud of her parahuman powers, and Annalisa suspected whatever superhero name she eventually chose, he'd be disappointed if it wasn't Halcónita. In spite of that, he wouldn't tolerate her using them wrongly, and he'd warned her many times what kind of consequences might come from such an act.

"No, Papi. They, uh, they tripped me. I fell and yelled at them." Annalisa continued to study her shoes. She knew she was lying, and hated that she was to her parents, but she didn't want to tell them the truth after she'd wound up working alongside the Culture Club to stop the bank robbery. She thought that would be rude.

"And?" Her mother stirred the soup and then laid the sandwiches on the grill sheet.

"And they gave me detention, and I'm very sorry. I won't do it again."

Her mother turned to look at her, fire in her eyes. "You better not, *mi hija*, or you'll see what my superpower is."

Annalisa sighed. She knew it was *super-grounding* and *super-taking-away-privileges*. "I promise, Mamá." She sat at the table and rested her chin on her hands, feeling like a baseball game that got rained out.

"Do you have homework over the weekend?" asked her father.

Annalisa thought it over. Did she? She didn't think so and repeated as much to him.

"I don't have any concrete work this weekend either. Maybe we could all go to the lake tomorrow. Closest thing to a beach in these parts."

"That sounds nice," said her mother. She flipped the sandwiches. "We could grill burgers."

Annalisa felt torn. A day spent at the lake sounded really awesome, but she also wanted to share her success at crime fighting with the rest of the Neighborhood Watch. Maybe it could be the beginning of some upgraded efforts to be real superheroes. She opened her mouth to say what she'd accomplished, but the doorbell interrupted her.

"That better not be someone selling something," said Annalisa's mom.

Her dad got up from the table and went to the front door to tell whoever it was they weren't buying, they'd already found Jesus, and they gave at the office. Annalisa heard him speaking to someone at the door, and he returned a moment later. "Annalisa, *sus amigas están aquí.*"

Her friends? Oh, of course, it had to be the rest of the Neighborhood Watch, over to hear the all the sordid details of how Annalisa had taken down the bank robber (with just a little help from the Culture Club). She hurried out to the front room and stopped short when she saw Brianna, Brittany, and Brooklyn standing in the doorway, smiling at her along with a severely-dressed woman who looked enough like them that she had to be their mother.

They all wore matching outfits.

Brittany stepped forward, her grin stretching from ear to ear. "Hi, Annalisa. We were wondering if you would like to come spend the night at our house. We have so much to talk about after this afternoon."

Brianna moved up beside her sister. "We'd love to have you over."

Brooklyn added, "I mean . . . yeah, totally."

The triplets' mother smiled at Annalisa and her parents, who'd followed Annalisa into the front room. "Hello, Mr. and Mrs. Torres. I'm Barb. The girls were really hoping Annalisa could come over tonight. They've got some tabletop games to play and we'll feed her dinner and breakfast. Is that all right?"

"Annalisa, you didn't say anything about spending the night at your friends' house," said Annalisa's mom. "I'm sorry, Barb. I didn't know about it. Of course she can spend the night. After all, you young ladies are the famous Culture Club and Annalisa does love her superpowers."

"But Mamá, you already made sandwiches—" began Annalisa.

"No worries. I'm sure your father is hungry enough to eat two." Annalisa's mom winked at Barb in a way that made Annalisa lose her appetite. "And it's not often we get a night to ourselves."

"Go pack your bag, Annalisa," said Brittany. "This is going to be so much fun!"

Feeling shell-shocked and confused, Annalisa went to her bedroom, as much to escape the unbelievable circumstances as to pack an overnight bag. What in the world was the Culture Club doing in her front room, inviting her over, acting like they'd been friends forever? She didn't trust them, especially after the kind of bullying they'd done earlier in the day that had gotten Annalisa into trouble. On the other hand, they'd been helpful in capturing the bank robber. In spite of her best efforts, Annalisa couldn't have done it all by herself. Plus, they'd come with their mom. Surely she wouldn't condone bullying. Maybe this was an overture from the triplets; a peace offering of sorts.

Annalisa had a small duffel bag she used for sleepovers at Wheels' house, and it only took her a minute to cram in a change of clothes, lightweight summer pajamas, phone charger, and her toothbrush. She wasn't the sort of person to assume the worst about others. She'd give the Culture Club the benefit of the doubt.

She returned to the front room to discover Brianna, Brooklyn, and their mother had left and only Brittany was still waiting for her. "The others are out in the car, waiting for us."

Annalisa's mom clapped a hand on her shoulder. "Go on, Annalisa. Don't keep your friends waiting." Annalisa looked up at her mom.

"No, you're not in any more trouble about today at school. We'll talk about that another time."

"I saw what you did today, *Halcónita*," said Annalisa's father. "*Muy valiente*. I'm proud of you." Despite his stern tone, Annalisa saw the sparkle of pride in her father's eyes. He'd called her brave. That meant a lot to her. She wanted so much for her parents to be proud of her as a superhero, and she'd finally made some strides toward reaching that place.

"What did she do today?" Annalisa's mom sounded suspicious.

Her dad held up his phone. "I'll show you, *mi amor*." He smiled once at Annalisa and then headed back into the kitchen.

Annalisa's mom paused before following him to tell Annalisa to be good and behave herself.

"I will, Mamá."

Annalisa's mom followed her dad into the kitchen, leaving Brittany and Annalisa alone in the front room.

"Look," said Brittany before Annalisa could ask what was going on. "We talked it over, and we think maybe we were wrong about picking on you. We decided to invite you over, you know, to make it up to you."

"I accept your apology," Annalisa said, even though she wasn't sure she'd actually gotten one from Brittany.

Brittany gave her a wide smile. "Good. Let's go. We're going to have a great time."

Annalisa followed her outside into the early evening. The sun was hanging low but it was a Friday, and many of the neighbors were sitting on their porches drinking iced tea or beers, watching their kids play or talking about baseball and soccer. The air smelled of grilled meat, cut grass, with just a hint of weed on the breeze. It was as close to a perfect late spring weekend evening, and Annalisa hoped that feeling would continue onward during her overnight stay with the triplets. If worst came to worst, she figured she knew her way around the neighborhood well enough to find her home, even in the dark.

It was quite some time later in the evening when she recalled she'd left her cape at home, still stuffed into her backpack.

Chapter Seven

The Culture Club triplets lived in a large house in the expensive part of town, an area where Breezy said you could get stopped by the cops if you didn't *look right*. Annalisa hadn't been in that neighborhood before, and she pressed her nose against the glass of Barb Arnold's SUV, looking at the large houses with their magnificently-sculpted yards and gardens.

Brittany sat in the front seat but kept leaning around to talk to Annalisa and her sisters. Brianna sat next to Annalisa, while Brooklyn had been relegated to the far back seat. She didn't seem to mind so much, as she kept elongating her neck so her head was between Brianna and Annalisa. At first it was creepy, but Annalisa was starting to get used to it. The Arnolds kept up their friendly chatter about what they were going to do once they got back to their house. Annalisa tried to nod and smile and interject occasionally into the conversation, but it was like trying to overpower an orchestra with a single violin.

At last, Mrs. Arnold pulled the SUV into a driveway and braked to a stop. Brittany and her sisters tumbled out of the car. Annalisa followed after them at a more leisurely pace, taking the time to look around at how the other half lived. She knew Mrs. Arnold was a fashion designer who was always jet-setting off to shows in New York, or Paris, or Shanghai. Her eye for the severe cuts and geometric shapes had earned her a place in the world of high-class fashion, and yet she kept her family in the small town where she'd begun instead of relocating to one of the hotbeds of the industry. Annalisa wondered why the Arnolds didn't move to New York, but was glad they didn't. Otherwise, when she was with Just Cause, she'd probably still have to deal with Brittany and her sisters.

The house sat up high on a hill, where it could overlook the less-wealthy neighbors below. The circular driveway had an offshoot leading to a four-car garage. The house looked like three floors plus a basement and a huge porch lined with planters and torch fixtures. The lawn must have been professionally maintained to look as smart as it did. Annalisa couldn't imagine living surrounded by such wealth, but the triplets rushed into the house like it was meaningless. Brittany turned back at the door. "Come on, Annalisa!"

"Go on, Annalisa," said Mrs. Arnold.

Annalisa shouldered her duffel bag and followed the triplets into the house. Inside, it was bright even though the sun was low in the sky, with lots of natural light coming in through high windows and skylights. Gleaming white walls and spotless carpet only made the place look even bigger than it already was. Polished wood accents were everywhere. Framed art hung on the walls, and carved wooden statuary sat in alcoves. A hardwood stairwell even wider than those in the school led to the upper floor. Annalisa looked up to see a chandelier of crystal overhead, sparkling in the sun. Soft classic pop music played from hidden speakers, quiet enough not to be distracting but persistent enough to fill the air nevertheless. Something delicious was cooking in the kitchen, and Annalisa wondered if it was Mr. Arnold's night to cook.

Ben Arnold was a field reporter for KTVG, and he'd built his reputation on the so-called heroics of his daughters. Any time they appeared in public, he made a point of covering it, while their mother managed them from the background. It made for a classic one-two punch of publicity that the Neighborhood Watch had never managed to defeat. Thinking of her friends made Annalisa feel guilty. She should have been hanging out with them on a Friday night, sharing her success against the bank robber. Instead, she was in the den of her mortal enemies, and she couldn't figure out what they were thinking.

She resolved to be more suspicious.

"You can just leave your bag on the floor there," said Brooklyn. "Carson will bring it down later."

"Who's Carson?" asked Annalisa.

Brooklyn shrugged. "The help."

Annalisa looked over at Mrs. Arnold but she was on her cell phone, gesticulating angrily and speaking in some foreign language.

"It's okay, Anna. Can we please call you Anna?" asked Brianna.

Annalisa shrugged. "I guess."

"Okay, Anna. Carson can take care of your bag for you. He's making dinner now. He's a great chef." Brittany tugged on Annalisa. "Come on, we want to show you the Club."

"I thought you were the Club." Annalisa walked through the house with the triplets, trying not to stare at the photos of Mrs. Arnold's award-winning outfit designs in the hall or the collection of media trophies in the stairs heading down to the basement.

"Mom and dad gave us the entire basement," said Brianna. "It's our superhero headquarters. We call it the Club."

"Because we're the Culture Club," added Brooklyn.

"Exactly. Don't your friends have like a tree house or something?" asked Brittany.

"No, it's—" Annalisa stopped as she exited the stairwell into a large, open basement that seemed to be everything she'd ever wanted in a superhero headquarters.

"Pretty awesome, huh?" said Brittany. "Come on, we'll show you around. Over here is where we practice fighting the bad guys."

One end of the basement looked like an actual training center. The floors, walls, and even the ceiling were padded. A couple of boxing bags hung from the ceiling, and there was a wooden training dummy, wrapped up in layers and layers of foam. Fake weapons, like whiffle bats and Nerf guns were hung on a rack along one wall beside a padded suit like what Annalisa had seen the victims wear in a TV show about training police dogs.

"Carson wears that suit for us when we need someone to beat up." Brooklyn laughed. "He doesn't mind, though. We're careful not to hurt him."

The middle of the headquarters was dominated by a big table with laptops at every seat and a giant flat screen television along the wall. The screen currently displayed a map of the town. Along one edge were feeds from all the local networks, as well as a box that looked like it was translating police dispatch calls. "When there's an emergency here in town, those emergency lights flash around the edges of the screen," said Brianna. "The software tells us what it is and where it is."

"Then all we have to do is show up," said Brittany. "But we're not going to do that tonight. Not with you here." She grinned. "The town's just going to have to get along without the Culture Club."

Brianna pointed to the far end of the headquarters. "That's where we'll sleep tonight.

That's our play area. Super comfortable. Big beanbag pillows that are like sleeping on air. Fuzzy blankets, even though it doesn't get cold down here. Tabletop games. Video games. It's awesome."

"We all have our own rooms on the top floor," said Brooklyn. "We're almost never there except to change our clothes. All the cool shit is down here."

Annalisa gasped. "I'm not allowed to say that. Are you?"

Brooklyn snickered. "No, but I do sometimes anyway, because I can."

"Aren't you worried about getting in trouble?"

"No. Mom almost never comes down here. She's not really into the whole superhero thing. Besides, she was talking to someone in Paris, which means she'll be busy for hours. It's just us. What do you want to do first?"

Annalisa looked around, stunned at everything she saw. If someone had asked her to describe her perfect superhero headquarters, it would have sounded a whole lot like what the Culture Club already had in their basement. "I . . . I don't know." Her stomach rumbled. "I am hungry, though. Are we going to eat soon?"

Brittany nudged her. "I'll find out. Watch this. You're going to love it. George?"

"Yes?" A disembodied voice came from the speakers around the huge television on the wall.

"Open a channel to the kitchen."

"Channel is open to the kitchen. Go ahead."

"Hey, Carson? How soon is dinner?" asked Brittany.

"I'll have it all wrapped up in about five minutes," said a cheerful voice. "What do you ladies all want to drink?"

The triplets all asked for Pepsi, so Annalisa did too, even though she preferred Coke. "Who's George?" Annalisa asked Brittany.

"George is like Siri, but for the Culture Club system. It's wired into the whole house. You can ask it anything. Go on."

Annalisa felt stupid. "Uh, George?"

"Yes?"

She didn't know what to ask. "What's, uh, what time is it?"

"It's seven forty-one."

"Thank you."

"You're welcome."

Brooklyn laughed. "You don't have to thank it. It's just a computer voice."

Annalisa shrugged. "I'm just being polite."

The triplets showed her their big pile of tabletop games. They had thousands of video games available on-demand, as well as movies, TV shows, and streaming music. They were just starting to narrow down what they wanted to do first when Carson arrived with their dinner.

Carson was a tall, muscular man with a gruff voice and dark stubble dotting his chin and cheeks. His hair was pulled up into a short ponytail up high, where a hipster would have a man-bun. He smiled at

Annalisa and she felt her cheeks get hot. He looked like a male model or an actor. He held a tray piled high with dinner fixings and beverages, and got right down to serving. "Ladies, tonight I've made you *croque-monsieurs*. They're grilled ham and gruyère sandwiches on brioche. As an accompaniment, I've made a tomato bisque with cracked black pepper and green onions. On the side you have panko-fried pickles and spicy bacon ranch dipping sauce. *Bon appetit!*" He laid the plates of food in front of the girls, opened their bottles of Pepsi for them, and bowed. "Please call me if you need anything else." He left.

Annalisa looked down at what was maybe the most amazing grilled-cheese sandwich she'd ever seen. The bread was a rich golden brown, more like a French toast than a regular piece of sliced bread. There was cheese both inside and on top of the sandwich, and the ham was a delicious addition. The soup was creamy and spicy without being too hot, although Annalisa pushed the green onions aside as being a little too weird for her. The fried pickles were astonishing, crunchy and bursting with salt and vinegar, tamed by the bacon ranch dressing.

Annalisa felt guilty all over again as she ate the delicious dinner, realizing it was a much more classy version of what her mom had made. Suddenly a grilled white-bread sandwich with individually-wrapped American cheese slices and canned tomato soup sounded really disappointing. Conversation slowed somewhat as the triplets inhaled their dinner, as if it wasn't anything special. Annalisa took her time eating, savoring the flavors and wondering if she could convince her mom to try making a grilled cheese the way Carson had.

"So, listen," said Brittany after washing down her sandwich with her Pepsi. "We had two main reasons for inviting you over tonight, Anna."

Annalisa grimaced at the shortened version of her name, which she'd never liked very much. At last, it seemed like she was going to get some answers to the triplets' unexpected behavior, and she was curious to find out the reasons why. "What are they?"

"Well, first, we wanted to apologize for messing with you." Brittany glanced at her sisters. Brianna and Brooklyn nodded in unison. "We were just having fun and didn't mean to get you in trouble."

"It's okay." Annalisa cleared her throat. "In the end, I guess it worked out for the best."

Brittany beamed. "And that leads me to the second reason we invited you over. We want you to join us."

Annalisa blinked. "Join you?"

"Join us. The team."

Brooklyn leaned over. "We want you to be part of the Culture Club."

Chapter Eight

Join the Culture Club?

Annalisa's immediate, knee-jerk response might have been to shout "No, never!"

Instead, she stared at her half-eaten sandwich and shuffled her feet beneath the table. "I'll, uh, I'll think it over."

"Look, I know we kind of got off on the wrong foot, but you have to admit we worked together really well today," said Brittany. "We caught the bad guy and everything."

"Yeah, a real supervillain. We took him down with teamwork," added Brianna.

"We couldn't have done it without you," said Brooklyn with a smile.

Annalisa wanted to say she already had a team, but she had to admit the Culture Club had a point. No matter how heroic she wanted to be, she couldn't have taken out the face-changing supervillain by herself. She'd needed the triplets' help, and they'd needed hers. The Neighborhood Watch hadn't been around. They were too slow to get there.

They were always too slow, it seemed. Annalisa could fly so much faster than the others. She was forever waiting for them to catch up. It was infuriating.

Maybe it wouldn't be the worst thing in the world to divide up her time between teams. Maybe it would keep the triplets from picking on the others. It might even be beneficial. They could make a giant super-team, like Just Cause in its heyday. Or they could be two allied teams that worked together when needed, like the Champions and Just Cause.

Carson came back down the stairs with a tray of desserts. "Who wants brownies and ice cream?"

"We do!" cried the triplets.

"They're the best brownies ever," added Brooklyn. "They've got caramel on them."

"Annalisa?" Carson held out a plate to her with a warm brownie on it topped with golden caramel and a scoop of vanilla ice cream melting around the edges.

"You won't be sorry," said Brittany.

Annalisa nodded. "Thank you."

"You're very welcome." Carson set the plate before her and then moved around the table to distribute similar plates to the triplets.

They devoured their brownies, delicious to the last swirl of ice cream dotted with chocolate crumbs. Annalisa sat back from the table. She didn't think she'd been so full since the previous Thanksgiving when she had two full plates of dinner plus a piece of pumpkin pie. She thought a nap might be in order.

"Do you guys want to paint our nails?" asked Brianna. The other triplets immediately agreed it was imperative to do so. Brooklyn stretched an arm all the way across their headquarters to grab a clear plastic box full of colors and the four girls had to sort through them until they found colors they all liked. The triplets all went for variations of red, but Annalisa decided upon the one purple they had in the box. She wanted to be different.

After painting their nails, the girls spent some time messing around with a costume designer program installed on their computers. "Look, we're not saying your costume isn't good," Brittany told Annalisa. "It's just that it's really, um, *rustic.*"

"Yeah, like something really old-timey. Like from the Eighties," added Brooklyn.

"Hey, let's all design new costumes." Brianna smiled at Annalisa. "Even you, Annalisa. In case you decide you want to join the Culture Club."

"The offer is still open," said Brittany.

Annalisa shrugged. In spite of her determination to be suspicious, the triplets had been pretty nice to her all evening. They'd taken care to include her in conversations and in deciding what to do next. They seemed like they genuinely wanted her to join their team, and somehow, she was actually considering it.

The triplets had some software on their system that had been designed by the same people who wrote software for Mrs. Arnold. It allowed them to upload pictures of themselves and then dress themselves in virtual superhero costumes that they could design. Brianna said once they settled on a design they could save it and send it to their mom's design studio and the people who worked there would create the costumes and then ship them back overnight.

"It's why we always have new costumes. Looking the same all the time is boring," said Brooklyn.

Brittany winked. "It's also why we always look so fashionable. We're, like, trend-setters. Mom has even adapted some of our designs for runway use. She's going to make superhero chic the next big thing in fashion.

Annalisa had seen some of what passed for high fashion on the internet. She wasn't too impressed with it. It all looked terribly uncomfortable and impractical. Brittany had her stand in an alcove with her arms out at her sides while lasers flashed all around her, making a 3D scan of her size. After a few minutes of processing and image rendering, there was a virtual Annalisa on the giant flat screen by the conference table. The girls—all of them, even Annalisa—laughed as Brittany spun the image around on all three axes.

Then Brittany moved to a different station at the table, as did the other girls. "Go ahead and try it out, Anna," said Brittany. "It's easy to start dressing yourself up once you get the hang of it. The app is easy to use, because our mom doesn't have patience for computers." Brianna and Brooklyn laughed and a moment later the triplets' own virtual likenesses appeared on the big screen.

Annalisa experimented a little with the app and they were right, it wasn't hard to use. It was like creating a character in a video game, except she could use a lot more details. The choices and color palettes were overwhelming. She wasn't really a graphic artist, and didn't have a good sense of what colors or styles went together. That was a side effect of homemade costumes: using only what one had on hand already to create.

Well, there was one thing she knew she liked, and after a bit of searching, a flowing cape appeared behind Virtual Annalisa.

Brittany lowered her hands from her keyboard, where she was designing a costume around a dark blue diagonal swoop design. "Anna, what are you doing?"

Annalisa shrugged. "Designing a costume, I guess."

"With a cape?"

"I like capes."

Brianna chimed in with "Capes are dumb."

Annalisa looked at her. "No, capes look awesome, especially when you're flying."

"I can't fly."

"And a cape would just get in the way of my powers," said Brooklyn.

"Capes are for, like, really old superheroes. Nobody wears one anymore." Brittany shook her head. "You need to update your look, Anna. Here, let us design something for you."

Over the next hour or so, the triplets worked on a new look and eventually arrived at a pair of hip-hugging shiny black pants tucked into blue ankle boots. The dark blue diagonal swoop Brittany had started with became a belly shirt with the swoop framed in white and highlighted in yellow. They added fingerless gloves of the same color as the ankle boots and swoop. Their concession to Annalisa's desire for a cape became a long, flowing black silk scarf. "That's the most we'll do," said Brooklyn. "Capes get in the way of everything. At least you can tuck a scarf around your neck enough that it's not going to get caught in stuff."

"It's not a bad look," said Annalisa. She had to admit that it actually looked pretty good on her virtual self on the screen. She didn't think she'd mind wearing it so much.

"It'd look awesome if we had, you know, boobs." Brianna laughed, and the others followed suit.

"I'm ordering them," said Brittany. "We'll have them by tomorrow. Then we can wear them to school on Monday."

Annalisa's smile faded. Was she really going to wear the same costume as the Culture Club? That was like conceding victory to them. No, she thought, she wasn't conceding anything. She didn't have to pick one team over the other. She could be a bridge between both of them. "Hey, maybe we could get costumes for the rest of the Neighborhood Watch. You know, so we look like we're all on the same side."

Brittany shrugged. "We'll see. We'd have to get them all over here to scan them."

"Mom doesn't like us to have more than one friend over at a time," added Brianna.

"It's distracting to her," said Brooklyn. She yawned and Annalisa realized they were already up past midnight. "You guys want to binge-watch *Rooftops*?"

The girls settled into comfortable beanbag chairs in the entertainment area of the headquarters and turned on the first episode of the popular vampires-werewolves-superheroes series. Annalisa had faithfully watched the entire first season at home, but there was something fun about rewatching it with her new friends. Were they friends? Yeah, she guessed they were.

Between the delicious food, the business of creating costumes, and the comfortably soft chair, Annalisa fell asleep before the werewolf vigilante made his first appearance.

Chapter Nine

Annalisa awakened early, as was her habit. The triplets were all curled up on other beanbag chairs, snoring softly. Annalisa had no idea what time it was down in the Culture Club's basement headquarters, but she didn't feel like she'd slept in. She wandered over to the conference table. "Uh, George?"

"Yes, Anna?" So the AI was going to call her that too? That at least was something she could change.

"First of all, call me Annalisa or La Capitána if I'm being a superhero. Second, what time is it?" Something on one of the peripheral monitors caught her eye. "And last, what does that flashing red light mean?"

"Okay, I'll call you Annalisa or La Capitána if you're being a superhero. Second, it's seven twenty-two. Last, the red light is an alert for the Culture Club of something requiring their attention."

"An alert . . . Why didn't you wake us up?"

"I was placed into Silent Mode for your overnight stay."

"But that's stupid!"

George didn't reply.

Annalisa sighed. What had she expected it to say? "Okay, George. What was the alert?"

A news video appeared on the big screen from the previous evening. The reporter broke the news that the parahuman bank robber stopped by the local teen superheroes The Culture Club had managed to escape from holding. Although the police had not released security video at the time of the broadcast, a nearby traffic camera had caught him in the act of stealing a police car to make his escape. His face was mid-transformation in the camera's view and his melting features were enough to put Annalisa off the idea of breakfast.

"Did they catch him?"

George opened a search window and the headlines almost screamed at her: *rogue parahuman on the loose, parahuman escapee still at large.*

"Dang it!" Annalisa checked her phone. She'd turned the sound off while eating. It was a common courtesy her mom insisted upon, but Annalisa was beginning to think would forever be a bad idea. She had multiple notifications flashing for text messages from everyone on the Neighborhood Watch, as well as notifications from Wheels' team app. While she and the Culture Club had been playing virtual dress-up, real crime had gone down. She started to text

Wheels to see if they had done anything about the robber, but then realized of course they hadn't. If they'd caught him, it would have been in the news. They had been just as ineffective as they always were. Besides, what could she tell Wheels? Certainly not the truth!

She'd have to figure out later what to tell the Neighborhood Watch. In the meantime, she could focus on the escapee and see if she could discover who he was and where he might have gone. She became solo absorbed in her research that she jumped when Brittany spoke beside her. "What are you doing?"

"Geez, Brittany, give me a heart attack."

"Sorry." Brittany yawned. "What is that?"

"That guy. The bank robber guy. He escaped." Annalisa couldn't help the mild accusatory tone that sneaked into her voice. "While we were playing dress-up."

Brittany folded her arms. "That's not our fault. We took him down and turned him over to the police. We can't help it if they can't do their jobs."

Annalisa didn't miss that it was now *we took him down*. Was she already on the team without even having any say in the matter?

Footsteps sounded on the stairs. At first Annalisa thought it might be Carson, but instead it was the triplets' father, reporter Ben Arnold, of the local station KTVG. "Who's not doing their jobs, Brittie? I sure hope it isn't me."

"Daddy!" Brittany squealed and flew across the room to embrace her father.

He gasped and chuckled. "Easy, there. You'll break my ribs." He peeked past her blonde head. "Is this her?"

Brittany nodded. "Daddy, this is Anna. She's our new teammate. She helped us take down the bank robber yesterday."

Annalisa wanted to shrink into her chair and disappear. Apparently she didn't have any say in the matter. She felt like correcting Brittany in front of her father would not only be rude, it would lead to even worse retribution from the Culture Club than shenanigans in the classroom.

Mr. Arnold came over to Annalisa and extended his hand. "Pleased to meet you, Anna. I'm Ben Arnold. I'd love to do an interview. The girls have had nothing but nice things to say about you and your powers."

The other two triplets stirred from where they sprawled on their beanbag chairs. "Oh hi, Dad," said Brianna.

"Hey, fam," said Brooklyn. "Can I go back to sleep now?"

"No, stupid," said Brittany. "Daddy wants to interview us. Hey George, are our new outfits here yet?"

"According to tracking information, they are on a truck for delivery this morning," said the AI.

"You have to wait until we have our new costumes," said Brittany. "We have one for Anna too."

"Ooh, breakfast! We should have breakfast first," said Brianna. "Is Carson here today or is he off?"

Mr. Arnold smiled. "He's upstairs, Brainy. I believe he's making French toast."

Brooklyn stretched an arm across the room to nudge Annalisa. "He makes the best French toast. Worth waking up for." She yawned. "Mostly."

"Tell you what, girls," said Mr. Arnold. "You enjoy your breakfast. I'll work up a question list for you and we'll shoot the interview after you all get changed. Sound good?"

"Sounds great," said the triplets in unison.

"Uh, yeah," added Annalisa. She almost felt like she'd been kidnapped. She wished Wheels was around to advise her. That thought made her feel even guiltier. She looked at her phone again, wondering what she should say to her friends. She needed time to think of something, but being around the triplets was working against her in that respect. Their bubbly excitement was exhausting to be around, and it made thinking of details difficult. Even at their arguing worst, the Neighborhood Watch had never made Annalisa feel like such a stranger. Maybe that was because they were all misfits in their own way, whereas the Culture Club were exactly the opposite. They were the trendy, popular kids, and Annalisa had no idea how to relate to them.

Instead of eating in their headquarters, the triplets decided they would eat in the kitchen. "We can't stay in the cave all the time, we'll turn into trolls, like Brooklyn." said Brianna.

"Speak for yourself, buttface," Brooklyn retorted, reinforcing her sister's statement by stretching her inhumanly-flexible face into a troll-like grimace.

Brittany looked at her sisters and smiled like an indulgent older sister. Annalisa wondered which of them had been born first. She'd always thought of them as three copies, each identical to the others, but she was starting to learn about the differences between them, and they were great enough she wondered how anybody had trouble telling them apart.

Brittany was the Leader-with-a-capital-L. She was a bit taller than the other two, with a little more muscle mass and definition in her arms and legs that might have been due to her powers. Likewise, her neck was a little thicker, her jaw a little squarer. When she said *jump*, her sisters obeyed her without argument (or in Brooklyn's case, not *much* argument). She had all the makings of becoming a true superhero, if not for her nasty streak. Well, Annalisa reasoned, maybe she'd grow out of it.

Brianna was the clown of the bunch. She liked cracking jokes and had the timing of a professional comic. It might have been because her powers were strictly mind-based. She tended to use humor to defuse situations instead of more violent means. She was the most slender of her sisters, almost a beanpole from shoulders to ankles. Her eyes sparkled all the time and her giggle was infectious. She was the only one who ever seemed to have a chance of changing Brittany's mind about anything.

Brooklyn was the sourpuss of the three, who had a perfect example of what Annalisa's mom called *resting bitch face*. She was always grouchy, and she seemed to resent the other two girls just a bit. Maybe it was because their powers didn't change their bodies in any way, while Brooklyn's deformed hers every time she used them. More than once, Annalisa saw Brooklyn lengthening her legs a bit so she would be as tall as Brittany, or even taller. Her hips were starting to develop the curves of womanhood, and although Annalisa knew all three girls wore bras, Brooklyn was the only one who really needed one.

Carson made fantastic French toast, as the girls kept reminding Annalisa. At first, she'd planned to be skeptical, even suspicious, but after she tasted her first bite of the pecan, caramel, and whipped cream topping, mixed with the lightest, fluffiest French toast she'd ever had, Annalisa was sold. It filled her up faster than she would have expected, and by the time she'd finished a second piece, she was thinking it was time for a nap to recover. Maybe she could beg off the interview and do it another time, after she'd had a chance to sleep off her breakfast and could be at the top of her game.

The doorbell rang and Brittany jumped out of her chair. "I bet that's our new costumes! I'll get them!" She flew out of the kitchen, her blonde hair fluttering behind her in a tangled mess. She returned a minute later with a box emblazoned with the *BASH Designs* logo on it, after Mrs. Arnold's company. "Costumes! Come on, you guys, let's get changed and try them out!"

Brianna pushed her plate away, leaving half her French toast uneaten.

Brooklyn shoveled the rest of hers into her mouth, leaving a trickle of whipped cream on her chin.

Annalisa sighed. Maybe she'd get to take a nap later. Then she brightened up. It wasn't everyday that she got to try on a brand new superhero costume.

Maybe it would be okay after all.

Chapter Ten

The costume looked even better than Annalisa had imagined it would. The swooping diagonal blue stripe with its yellow outline was dramatic and exciting, the way a superhero costume ought to look. She didn't really have hips yet, the same as Brianna, so she had to hitch up the shiny black pants regularly to keep them from falling. The white scarf looked weird to her, but she hadn't ever worn a scarf before and figured it might take some getting used to.

She and the triplets examined themselves before a floor-to-ceiling, wall-to-wall in the dressing room. The fact that the triplets actually had a *dressing room* was taking some adjustment on Annalisa's behalf. They turned around to look at themselves over their shoulders, then twisted first one way and then the other.

"What do you think?" Brittany asked her sisters.

Brianna shrugged. "It's better than being covered in that glittery crap mom likes."

Brooklyn likewise shrugged. "All I can stretch in this are my arms. And my ankles, I guess, which is just weird."

Brittany turned to face Annalisa. "What do you think, Anna?"

Annalisa studied herself in the mirror for almost a full minute before answering. "I like it," she said, although even saying so she still wasn't sure. If nothing else, she thought, she looked more like a superhero than she ever had with the mismatched outfits she'd managed to put together from stuff buried in her closet. She wished she had a cape.

She didn't feel super without one.

A knock came at the dressing room door. "Everybody decent?" asked Mr. Arnold from behind it.

"Yes, Daddy," said Brittany.

He poked his head into the room. "I've got the cameras set up downstairs in your headquarters. Come on down and we'll do the interview."

Brittany grinned at Annalisa. "Come on, Anna. This is your time to shine."

"It's just an interview," said Annalisa.

"It's more than that. It's letting the people out there get to know you. Letting them trust you. It's really important. We want them to call us when they need us. That's how we help." Brittany nudged her out of the dressing room.

"Besides, being famous is the best," said Brianna. "People are always giving you stuff. Daddy said he's working on a big en . . . erden . . . what is it? That deal thingie?"

"Endorsement," said Brooklyn. "Read a fricking book once in awhile, dumbbutt."

"Dad!" protested Brianna.

"Brookie, don't call your sister names." Mr. Arnold didn't turn around to look as he went down the stairs to the headquarters.

Brianna showed Brooklyn her middle finger behind Mr. Arnold's back. Brooklyn retorted by stretching hers way out and waggling them back at Brianna, along with her tongue flapping like a dog's.

The interview wasn't at all what Annalisa had expected. There were three cameras set up on tripods in the basement, along with some lights that were so bright they almost made her eyes water. She thought Mr. Arnold would ask a couple of questions and her answers would be short and the whole thing would take maybe a minute or two. On the news, it seemed like interview segments never lasted very long. Instead, he drew her and his daughters into a lengthy conversation on topics ranging from school to their home lives. Yes, eventually he brought up superheroes, the bank incident, and Annalisa's newfound relationship with the Culture Club. At first, she'd tried to be guarded in her answers, but eventually Mr. Arnold drew things out of her and she didn't even realize what all she'd said.

Finally, Mr. Arnold checked the clock on his phone and nodded. "I think we're done for now, Anna. Thank you so much for giving me the opportunity to speak with you. I've got some great footage. You're a natural when it comes to speaking to the camera, like Brittany. I suspect you'll have a long and storied career as a public superhero." He winked at her. "And I certainly hope it's as a member of the Culture Club."

"Uh, thank you," said Annalisa. She felt shell-shocked, like she'd been hit with three consecutive pop quizzes in Math, Science, and Geography. She checked her own phone and was dismayed to discover she'd forgotten to charge it. "What time is it, anyway?"

"Almost noon," said Brianna. "You're going to stay for lunch?"

It was a tempting offer, given the food Carson had already prepared for them, but Annalisa shook her head. "No, I need to head home. I've, uh, I've got homework to do this weekend."

"Homework? That's so boring." Brittany turned up her nose in disdain. "You don't really have to do it, you know."

"What do you mean? Of course I do."

Brittany glanced over at her father's departing form as he climbed the stairs back to the main floor. "Listen, we've got everyone at that stupid school wrapped up tight. There's not a teacher there who would dare give us a bad grade. We're the darlings of Malley Middle School."

"Most schools don't have a single parahuman, and Malley's got a whole team. Like Daddy says, any publicity is good publicity." Brianna grinned. "And he knows publicity."

"Homework is stupid," was Brooklyn's only addition to the conversation.

"You mean you guys don't do it?" asked Annalisa, aghast at the thought. "But what about your grades?"

"Who cares? We've got parahuman powers!" Brittany raised herself into the air and spun around once. "We patrol the school. We keep the vandals from spray painting the walls and tagging in the bathrooms."

"Look at where the school is in town. Look at the kind of kids who go to it. Somebody might have burned it down already if not for us," said Brianna, who had lost her joking demeanor.

Annalisa snorted. "Nobody's going to burn down the school."

"Of course not. Not while we're there to keep an eye on things," said Brittany.

"It's a mighty nice school," added Brianna. "Be a real shame if something happened to it."

"That's why we don't do homework," said Brittany with a smile. "We're too busy, too important."

"I'm not important enough not to do homework."

Brianna laughed. "After Daddy's feature airs, you will be."

Annalisa shrugged. "Still, I need to get it done, or I'll be grounded."

Brooklyn stretched her arm past her sisters to pat Annalisa's shoulder. "Someday, you won't have to worry about that."

Annalisa found herself weakening in the face of the triplets' combined effort. The truth was that she didn't actually have any homework to do. She needed to be away from the Culture Club's constant, three-pronged attack. She needed the comfort of her teammates—her *real* teammates. One in particular, she thought, picturing Breezy's cheerful grin. "Well, uh, today I have to, uh, worry about it."

Brittany shrugged. "Okay, I guess that's cool. You can go home, but you have to come back tomorrow."

"What's tomorrow?"

"*Sunday training!*" shouted all three triplets.

"That's where we get to use all that stuff at the other end of our headquarters," said Brittany. "It's a Combat Simulation Chamber, just like Just Cause has."

Annalisa glanced over at the beat-up training dummies and boxing bags. Somehow, she didn't think Just Cause's training was anything like the Culture Club's. Still, it would be better than nothing. She'd actually get to hit something instead of just pretending, like she had to when she was training with the Neighborhood Watch. "I'll think about it."

"You'll be here. I know it," said Brianna. "What else are you going to do? Watch YouTube? Chores?"

Annalisa shrugged. "Like I said, I'll think about it."

"Do you want us to have Daddy take you home? Mom's working with the door shut, and that means we're not supposed to bother her," said Brittany.

"No, that's okay. I'll fly." Annalisa lifted herself a foot off the ground, as much to remind herself that she *could* fly as to show it to the triplets. "I know my way home."

"If you fly, you have to wear your new costume." Brittany folded her arms. "And no cape. It would totally ruin the look and everything."

"All right, no cape."

The girls headed up the stairs to the main floor. As Annalisa shouldered her backpack, Carson came out of the kitchen with a black apron tied around his waist and a spot of some kind of red sauce on one cheek. "Oh, you're leaving? I was hoping you'd stay for lunch, Ms. Torres. I'm making enchiladas."

Annalisa smiled at him. "Sorry, Carson. Yeah, I'm going."

"She'll be back tomorrow," said Brittany in a tone that brooked no discussion. "For Sunday Training."

"Maybe." Annalisa turned to look at the triplets. "I'll think it over."

"You'll be here. You wouldn't ditch us. We're your teammates, and you're ours." Brooklyn nodded as if the matter were settled.

"Bye." Annalisa's uneasiness and dread threatened to overwhelm her into tears. Somehow she'd gotten railroaded into the

Culture Club, and she didn't know how she was going to extricate herself.

She needed to leave.

She needed her friends. Her real friends.

She flew away.

Chapter Eleven

Annalisa returned home from the triplets' house. Her folks were heading off to the store as she came in and they reminded her to do her chores and homework before she went to hang out with any of her other friends. Chores were easy, especially when she hadn't been home the night before. Her bed was still made, and her dirty clothes were already in her hamper. She didn't play with toys so much anymore, so her floor was already picked up as well. Her only other real chore was to unload the dishwasher, which she hated, but she made herself do it because she felt like she needed some grounding in the real world after spending a day in close proximity to the Culture Club.

Once dishes were put away, she thought she'd try to get a little ahead on the chore-karma list and did her best to load the dishwasher with her folks' breakfast dishes. She wasn't sure she did it right, but she figured the attempt would be worth it, whether the end results were success or failure.

Since she didn't have any homework, she sat down and read through another chapter of Sunstorm's book on parahuman combat. When she was done, she read it again to try to get more of the info to stick in her mind. By then, her folks had returned from the store and she asked for and received permission to go hang out with her friends. She was going to fly over to Wheels' house, but first she had to decide what she was going to wear.

She looked critically at the costume the Culture Club had given her. It just felt . . . wrong. It looked great and everything, and when she wore it, she looked more like a superhero than she ever had with her t-shirt and cape. She held it up against her and looked in her mirror. It didn't look like her. It was someone else with her face, like the guy who'd been able to change his appearance who'd tried to rob the bank. She threw the costume on the bed and dug through her backpack until she found her cape. It seemed so ratty and pedestrian compared to the fancy bodysuit the triplets had given her. Somehow, wearing it didn't seem right anymore either. The way she felt was like being lost in the supermarket.

She pulled on her superhero t-shirt and some shorts, but left the clunky boots and gloves in the box at the foot of her bed, and the cape got hung up on the peg on her door beside her bathrobe. Maybe she'd wear it later, but for now, she'd just be plain old Annalisa Torres instead of La Capitána.

A few minutes of flying across town and she landed in front of the Neighborhood Watch headquarters. She couldn't help but notice how run-down everything looked. It was in the middle of a scrap-yard. All the devices Wheels had built that sat on the roof of the beat-up Winnebago weren't much better than the junk from which they were built. And dirty! Everything was so dirty.

Then she shook her head in disbelief. How quickly the Culture Club had turned her against her friends, her *real* friends. The Neighborhood Watch was her team, not those triplets in their rich mansion in the good part of town. Her friends were inside that Winnebago, with as many smiles as smudges, and she wasn't going to let one night with Brittany, Brianna, and Brooklyn change any of that.

She sauntered in through the door. "Hey, guys!"

The rest of the team was indeed gathered in the Neighborhood Watch headquarters. Breezy must have finally gotten his costume laundered, for he was wearing it, his blue cape wrapped around him like a poncho. Rascal's demon mask sat on top of his head while he ate a bag of chips. Crumbs decorated his chin. Hothead had his feet propped up on the wall in one corner, his nose buried in his phone.

Wheels glared at Annalisa. "Well, look who finally decided to grace us with her presence."

Annalisa blinked, taken aback. "What's that supposed to mean?"

"First you go off to play superhero all by yourself. Then you team up with the Culture Club. The *Culture Club*, Annalisa! They might as well be our sworn archenemies. And now you're all buddy-buddy with them."

Hothead glanced up from his phone. "I'm surprised you even came back."

"Of course I came back! You guys are my friends, not them. They're just a bunch of rich jerks with parahuman powers."

"Rich jerks," said Wheels. "I guess that makes us the poor ones."

Breezy shrugged. "Well, we sure ain't rich."

"And not all of us are jerks," added Hothead.

Rascal raised his hand without looking up. "I am."

"Yeah, we know," said Wheels. "So what's the deal, Annalisa?"

"The deal is there's no deal. You guys, I'm one of you. I'm on the Neighborhood Watch. Wheels . . . Aighleigh, we started it together, you and me. I'm not going to walk away from that."

"Or fly," said Hothead. "What? She flies." His voice turned wistful. "I wish *I* could fly."

"What happened Friday night? I mean, what really happened?" asked Wheels. "I've seen the news stories and that lame shaky-cam one guy posted on YouTube, but that's all anyone's shared. You were there. How did it go down?"

Annalisa dutifully recounted the events of her stopping the bank robbery, beginning with her discovery of the security guards taped up inside the construction dumpster and ending with her punching out the would-be robber. "You guys wouldn't believe it. I mean, I knocked that guy out. It was all like *boom*—done." Annalisa slapped her hands together like she was brushing crumbs off them.

"That's cool," said Rascal. "I wish that dude with the camera phone had known how to hold his stupid hand still. Hashtag shaky-cam, right?" He held up a fist and Breezy bumped it.

"So you just happened to find a bank robber?" Wheels looked glum.

"I guess I was just lucky." Annalisa didn't back down. She felt like Wheels was looking for some reason, any reason to start a fight, and she didn't want to play that game. "I did call you guys, you know. It's not like I was all planning to, like, be a lone wolf. You're my team. Not the Culture Club. I can't help it if you weren't close enough to help out."

"Lucky for you the Culture Crap was." Wheels spun her chair to turn her back to Annalisa. "Convenient."

"I can't help that they were there. Maybe their mom had a thing to do over there. They're rich. I don't know what they do with their days." Annalisa stomped her foot hard enough to make the Winnebago quake. "But if they hadn't been there, I probably couldn't have stopped the guy."

Wheels didn't turn around. "You know he escaped, right?"

"That's not my fault. He's a supervillain. The police should have done a better job." Wheels turned around and opened her mouth to say something but Annalisa was faster. "I don't have Deep Six on speed dial, Aighleigh."

"Yeah, whyn'tcha lay off, Wheels?" Breezy's lazy voice drifted across the Winnebago, making Annalisa feel a little better. "She ain't the bad guy here. It's the dude who tried to rob the bank."

Wheels sighed. "I'm sorry. I guess I'm just mad that we didn't get to help. After all this time we've been trying to do some real good, and the first chance we get, we blow it."

"We didn't blow it," said Annalisa. "Listen, Mr. Arnold . . . you know, the reporter? He's the triplets' dad. He interviewed me. I talked a lot about the Neighborhood Watch. You guys. My friends." She smiled. "It might be on as early as five o'clock tonight." An idea occurred to her and she pulled out her phone. "In fact, I'll find out when it's on. We can all watch it. You'll see. We're going to be famous."

Wheels finally cracked a smiled and rolled her chair across the floor toward Annalisa. "You really think so?"

Annalisa texted Brittany. *Hey when is ur dads interview?*

Brittany texted back a minute later. *He says lead story 5 pm & again at 10.*

Cool thx.

"It's on in like an hour," Annalisa said. "Can we watch it in here?"

Wheels nodded. "Yeah, I've got a cable spliced into the neighbor's wire."

"Isn't that, like, illegal?" asked Hothead.

Rascal snickered into his hands. "Totally."

Wheels glared at him. "It might be, if my dad didn't already have cable."

"Then why you stealin' it from the neighbor?" asked Breezy.

"He's got a better package." The other laughed at Wheels' admission. "Also, I overheard him call me Meals on Wheels once, so he's a jerk."

"I guess that makes it okay," said Annalisa. She opened a drawer. There were several plastic-wrapped envelopes still inside. "Who wants popcorn?"

Over the next hour, while they waited for the news to come on, the five friends snacked on popcorn, drank Mexican Cokes, and discussed what they would do with their upcoming fame.

Rascal said he wanted to take TeamRascal big. "Like, TV big," he said. "I'd have feeds from all over."

"And then you'd just skateboard over to take care of whatever came up?" asked Hothead.

"Well, yeah!"

"Now me? I'd want to find some science types. You know, real nerds. Figure out how to amp up my powers. Just catching my hair on fire is lame. Imagine if I could do my whole body."

Wheels giggled. "We'd have to fireproof the Winnebago, especially if you get mad."

A single spark shot up from Hothead's hair, like from a popping log in a campfire. It went out almost immediately but just the same, Annalisa's hand strayed toward their one fire extinguisher.

"Me? I'd have pizza every day." Breezy patted his belly and smiled.

"Every day?" asked Rascal. "Dude, you'd weigh, like, a ton."

"I could still fly."

"Everyone would call you Blimpie," said Annalisa. "Don't do that."

"How 'bout you, Wheels? What would you do?" asked Breezy.

"I might go talk to Hothead's nerds. I just want to run again. That was the best feeling in the world."

Everyone was quiet for a few minutes after that.

Annalisa was the one who finally broke the silence. "I want to be the best superhero I can be. Not the best ever. Just the best I can be. I don't care about the fame. I'd do it in the dark of night with a mask if that was what made me the best."

Breezy fist-bumped her. "Word."

Wheels picked up a remote and turned on a flatscreen TV. "Let's watch the news, you guys."

Chapter Twelve

As she sat through the short feature Mr. Arnold had produced, Annalisa became more and more horrified. She'd expected it to be every question Mr. Arnold had asked, and all of her answers. Her answers were still there, but they had been edited so they were shorter, and often taken out of context to what she'd meant to say. The questions were different too. It was like Mr. Arnold had filmed an entirely different set of questions and then jumbled up Annalisa's replies to make the interview entirely about the Culture Club and Annalisa joining it. Every single one of her mentions of the Neighborhood Watch had been erased.

It not only made her look like she was a solitary superhero invited to join the Culture Club, it looked like it was what she'd wanted most in the world.

By the third question Hothead's hair was smoldering as he stood and muttered that he had to go outside. He stood just beyond the Winnebago door, watching the interview from his vantage point, and his hair burned as bright as a lantern on a dark night.

"And last but not least, Anna . . ." The way Mr. Arnold said her name made her want to crawl under the headquarters and stay there for days, like a stray cat. "Will you and the rest of the Culture Club be working to recapture the parahuman bank robber who recently escaped police custody?"

"I can't wait to get started," said Annalisa on the screen with a big grin. Annalisa clenched her fists. She'd said that when he asked if she was excited about going to the Hero Academy.

"Thank you, Ben," said the news anchor. "After the break, Perd will bring us the weather and tell us about some even hotter temperatures on the way next week. We'll see you in ninety—"

The TV went dark and Wheels lowered the remote. Annalisa felt her ears burning all the way to the tips, and a trickle of sweat rolled down her back. Everyone was staring at her. "That's not what I said!"

"Sure looked like it to me," said Rascal. The anger in his face matched the demon's visage of his plastic mask.

"No, I mean, I did say those things, but they changed the questions."

"Get out." Wheels pointed at the door. "Get out of our headquarters, Annalisa. Go be with your stupid Culture Club instead. We don't want you here."

"Aighleigh, please! They changed everything around. I talked about you guys and how great you were in the interview. They took all of that out and changed the questions."

Wheels' face showed her immediate fury, but even beneath that, Annalisa could see how badly her friend had been hurt. "You never should have gone over there in the first place. You shouldn't have let them interview you. They're bullies. They hate us. You shouldn't have been hanging around with the enemy."

"Hey, I mean, that's a little harsh, ain't it, Wheels?" Breezy raised his hands in supplication but Wheels was having none of it.

"No. All they do is try to make us look dumb, and Annalisa thinks they're right and that she's better than us."

Annalisa's mouth fell open in shock. "I don't think that!" she managed to say. "You guys are my friends, my team."

"Doesn't look like that from where I'm sitting," said Rascal. "I say we put it to a vote. We're a team." He raised his hand. "I say she's out."

Wheels' hand went up without a moment's hesitation. "Out."

Breezy didn't move. "No, she's one of us. She's our friend. Why you bein' this way, Wheels?"

Annalisa turned to give him a grateful smile but when she did, she saw Hothead standing in the door with his hair smoldering, his hand raised as well. "Really, Cole?"

"I know what I saw. And it wasn't just me. We all saw it. Everybody who watched the news saw it, Annalisa. Everybody thinks you're on the Culture Club now."

"Three to two," said Wheels. "Get out, and don't come back. The Neighborhood Watch doesn't need you anymore. We'll find someone else to do what you can do." She folded her arms. "Or we'll just be four."

Tears streamed down Annalisa's cheeks. It wasn't at all the outcome she'd envisioned. She thought she'd have the chance to bridge the gap between the Neighborhood Watch and the Culture Club, to make a *real* super-group from both teams. Instead, everything had fallen apart before her eyes because she'd been unwilling to see beyond the momentary fame of busting a real-live supervillain. She was either going to have to really join the Culture Club or go it alone. The former seemed like an untenable position, while the latter sounded about as much fun as the stomach flu.

She turned and pushed her way past Hothead and staggered down the Winnebago ramp and into the yard beyond. When she looked back at the Neighborhood Watch headquarters, she saw the remaining four heroes watching her from the windows and doors. Breezy gave her a sad smile and slow wave from the window. At least he didn't hate her, but the looks of disgust coming from Hothead and Wheels were more than enough to show her how they really felt. Rascal's mask hid his face, but she could sense the disappointment coming off him by the way he stood with his arms crossed, judging her.

Annalisa, no longer feeling like La Capitána— or any kind of superhero for that matter—turned away from her former friends and flew away.

She didn't really pay attention to where she was going, just drifted aimlessly over the heart of downtown. If she was a grim vigilante type, like White Fang in *Rooftops*, she could lurk and mope atop a tall building with stone gargoyles and stuff, but her town didn't have anything taller than six stories. Even if it did, she was a little scared of heights, and flying that high made her feel like throwing up. "Some superhero," she said with a sniffle. "Can't even fly right."

She wondered what the real superheroes would do. She was willing to bet Mustang Sally hadn't ever gotten kicked out of Just Cause because of an interview. If only things had gone differently . . . but that was a stupid thought, she told herself. Things hadn't gone differently. She had to accept the consequences of what had happened and carry on.

Still, she felt like hitting something, and when she flew over the remains of the building on West Tenth that was being demolished, those feelings got the better of her.

Her town wasn't big enough to have any real skyscrapers, so there wasn't a need to do the whole building-implosion thing she'd seen videos of online. Instead, companies took down an old building in the rare occasions they needed to do so by the use of a big excavator with hydraulic jaws on it. She'd seen her dad drive one before and it was terrifying and exhilarating.

The West Tenth demolition site was abandoned, of course, being a Saturday evening. The building was halfway down, with the excavator parked safely off to one side with its monstrous jaws closed and resting upon the ground. Rubble of the building's top floors surrounded the remaining three and Annalisa figured that they'd have the rest of it down by Monday.

She decided not to make them wait that long.

She flew down to the site and found a piece of steel. It was three times taller than her and heavy enough that she grunted with effort as she dragged it out from its pile. One end of it was twisted and bright with scarring where the hydraulic shears had snipped through it. It would be sharp enough to slice right through her clothes and her skin. She knew she was tougher than normal kids, but didn't want to cut herself so she held it by the other end. She hefted it, testing its weight, and figured she could get a pretty solid swing with it. And since she could fly, she could get out of the way of anything that fell faster than if she ran.

Kick her out of the Neighborhood Watch?

She swung her makeshift crowbar at the side of the building. It shivered with the impact and a big chunk of the wall collapsed down in a choking pile of dust. It felt really good to cut loose with her strength in a way she never had before. A savage grin spread across her face as she growled and struck the building again, and again, and again. If it had been alive, it would have been begging for mercy from her vicious onslaught, but instead, it collapsed in relative silence except for the groaning of overstressed steel and the crunch of broken bricks.

It only took her a few minutes, and when she was done, the building's bottom three floors had joined the pile of rubble. She threw down her pry-bar, now twisted and bend, and slapped at the dust caking her arms and clothing. The site dropped away beneath her as she flew into the sky, thinking she'd head home for a bath. She felt better, having worked off her frustrations. She was still mad at her friends, or perhaps her ex-friends, for throwing her off the Neighborhood Watch.

She'd show them.

Chapter Thirteen

Annalisa ended up accepting the triplets' offer to come back to visit them for their Sunday Training regimen, which turned out to be one of the best workouts Annalisa had ever had. They began with yoga, which Annalisa had never done before. Apparently it made people fart, because their stretches often devolved into giggles as one or the other of them let one go. Still, it loosened up her muscles so when Annalisa went to work with Brittany, she felt stronger than ever. They had a weight machine on a thick concrete pad in one corner of the basement that had smaller weights for Brianna and Brooklyn, who didn't like strength training, and weights in five-hundred pound increments for Brittany and Annalisa. Annalisa wouldn't have known how to use any of the various weight machines if it wasn't for the personal trainer the triplets' mother had hired for them. Her name was Sujin and she was meaner than a junkyard dog, Brianna had whispered to her.

Annalisa actually thought Sujin was pretty cool. She spent a lot of time with Annalisa, teaching her the proper ways to stretch, to lift weights, and to run. "Why do I have to run?" Annalisa asked. "I can *fly*."

"Flying is weak," Sujin said. "You're not using a single muscle when you do it. Do you even get tired when you fly?"

"No. I mean, I don't know. I've never flown long enough to find out."

"Do you get tired when you fight? Or lift extremely heavy weights?"

"I've, uh, never really been in a fight."

"You'll get tired. Your muscles will start burning lactic acid. Your body works the same whether you can bench-press fifty pounds or five thousand. If you don't work on your stamina and conditioning, you *will* get tired, and that might be the difference someday between saving someone's life or letting them die. Do you understand?"

Annalisa nodded, her eyes wide.

"Now *run!*"

Annalisa ran, along with the triplets, on a winding path around the house, across the tennis court where they had to jump over the net, climb up and over the fence, then do it all over again. Annalisa found climbing was a lot harder when she didn't use her flying power at all. The one time she gave herself a little boost, Sujin spotted it immediately and made her climb it again while the triplets waited.

After they were good and tired, Annalisa and the triplets got to enjoy smoothies made by Carson during a fifteen minute break. Then Sujin left and turned them over to a soft-spoken Slovakian man named Marek who trained them in their specific powers. He had Brooklyn working on flattening her limbs enough to reach past the edges of a sealed box to unlock it from the inside after finding her way through the three-dimensional maze contained within it. Brianna got to practice opening locks with her mind, starting with padlocks and then moving to handcuffs. Later, she worked on pressing the keys of a keyboard while blindfolded and bound.

Marek went with a much more direct approach for Brittany and Annalisa. He had them square off in a ring, their hands clasped, and ordered them each to try to push the other out of the ring. It turned out Brittany and Annalisa had similar strength levels as neither had a particular advantage. Annalisa found herself struggling to keep her temper back as she strained against Brittany. For so long she'd detested the Culture Club and all it stood for, but now that she had no place else to turn as a superhero, she was actually enjoying herself.

Their training session ended with a mock battle, directed by Marek. Annalisa was taken down quickly by the triplets' effective teamwork, but afterward, Marek said she was only inexperienced, not a bad fighter. He had a lot he could teach her and was looking forward to their next session, and honestly, so was Annalisa. It helped that Marek looked kind of like a movie star.

After their training, the triplets had Annalisa join them at their pool, and for the next three hours they lounged around the pool, soaking up sunshine, and eating fajitas that Carson cooked for them on the poolside grill.

"This is really great, huh?" Brittany said around a mouthful of barbacoa. "We do this every Sunday. Now you can, too."

Annalisa smiled as she sipped her lemonade. It was great, the way the triplets trained, the way they lived. It was the fantastic life she'd always thought superheroes should have. Only occasionally did stray thoughts of the Neighborhood Watch cross her mind, and then she'd frown as she remembered the way they'd treated her. Maybe the Culture Club was right and they weren't ever going to amount to anything.

Then she remembered how the triplets had treated *her* up until the weekend when she'd helped them to gain even more media exposure. Even now, when she was supposed to be part of their group, more often than not she was separated from the three sisters. Sometimes it wasn't any more than sitting on the other side of the table, or swimming while they were lounging in the poolside chairs. Just when Annalisa was starting to feel like she'd been excluded by the triplets, they'd call her over and she'd be treated to a barrage of conversation, questions, and girly chatter. It was overwhelming, and she grew to enjoy those moments of quiet solitude.

Eventually the afternoon turned into early evening and Annalisa's skin had turned a darker shade of brown from spending half the day by the pool. The triplets had applied sunscreen every twenty minutes to protect their fragile, pale skin, but even so, all three of them had pink spots on their noses and ears. Carson piled some wood in an iron-lined firepit and lit it to ward off the chill that the evenings still brought as it wasn't yet full summer. "Annalisa, will you be staying the night? I'm sure the Arnolds would love to have you."

"Please stay, Annalisa," said Brianna. "We've got so much to talk about what with school ending in only two weeks."

"We have permission to start patrolling. I mean, like, *really* patrolling, once we're done with classes." Brittany grinned.

"It's easier when we don't have to get permission from five different pairs of parents, you know?" Brooklyn stared into the flames. "You cool with it?"

"I don't know. I'll have to ask." Suddenly, Annalisa realized she could get out of it if she wanted. All she had to do was tell them her parents had denied her permission to go on patrol. Dang it, though, that was what she *wanted* to do. She'd even talked about it with the Neighborhood Watch. How were they going to ever stop crimes from happening if they didn't go out on the streets to seek it out? "How are you going to patrol, though?"

Brittany leaned in like she was telling a secret. "Mom is buying us a car for our graduation. We've already got a name for it. The Clubmobile. It's going to be our rolling headquarters for when we're on patrol. Carson's going to drive it. Everyone will see it and go, *there goes the Culture Club, they're so awesome.*"

It was such an unexpected announcement that Annalisa could only stammer, "Wh-what kind of car?"

"We don't know, but we're pretty sure it will be a limo of some kind," said Brianna.

"Because we're worth it." Brittany laughed.

"Eh." Brooklyn didn't sound as impressed, but Annalisa had learned that was a typical Brooklyn response to anything.

"So you're going to stay tonight, then?" Brianna asked.

"No, I really think I need to head home. It's a school night."

Brittany's snort made it clear how little she thought of that excuse. "You're in the Culture Club now. You don't need to worry about stuff like that."

"Well, uh, listen, it's going to take my folks a little time to come around." Annalisa knew she was making excuses, but she didn't know how to tell Brittany the truth that she was feeling overwhelmed by how fast everything was changing for her. It was like all her dreams were coming true in exactly the way she didn't want them to, and she didn't know how to deal with it. "Give it some time, okay?"

Brittany shrugged. "Your loss. We'll see you in the morning." And just like that, Annalisa knew she'd been *dismissed*. It was like she wasn't even by the pool any longer as far as the triplets were concerned. At least when the Neighborhood Watch had cut her loose, Breezy had the common decency to watch her go, and even wave. The triplets were already pestering Carson about whether he was going to make them s'mores before or after dinner.

Annalisa gathered up her things and flew home.

Chapter Fourteen

By Monday, the news of her joining the Culture Club had clearly made its way throughout the school's social media grapevine, and Annalisa had become the newest sensation of Malley Middle School. The triplets had insisted—*insisted*—she wear her costume to school on Monday, even though that was something she'd never done before. She felt silly and self-conscious when she got off the bus, but not one person teased her about her new outfit.

She saw Wheels in the school's circle drive, her wheelchair getting lowered by the short bus she rode. Annalisa hurried over, hoping to apologize and maybe find her way back into her friend's good graces. "Aighleigh! Hey, Wheels!"

Wheels turned to look over her shoulder, saw Annalisa's new costume, and sniffed in disdain. "Do I know you?" She touched a lever by her left hand and her wheelchair roared away in a cloud of dust, heading for the school entrance.

Annalisa bowed her head. It wasn't going to be as simple as she'd hoped. But then she clenched her fists. She was La Capitána, and she wasn't going to be defeated as easily as that. Before she could go after Wheels, a couple of younger students pushed in front of her. "Can we have your autograph?" asked one of them.

"Me first!" shouted the other.

"Uh, yeah, of course." Annalisa carefully wrote out her superhero name in cursive, the way her mom had taught her. The girl whose notebook she signed grinned like she was meeting a famous movie star instead of a middle school superhero. She signed the other girl's notebook.

A teacher who had never once paid the least bit of attention to her waved and smiled. "Hey, Anna. Saw you on the news. Great job stopping the bank robbery."

"Oh, uh, thanks."

Hothead walked past her, not even bothering to glance her way. "Too bad the robber got away," he muttered, soft enough that nobody else would hear it but her.

"That's not fair, Cole," said Annalisa, but he was already heading into the building.

She felt like crying. Was this her new life? Idolized by some and loathed by others?

"Hey, Anna, here we are!" Brittany's strident voice carried across the parking lot.

Annalisa turned to see the Culture Club striding across the cement like they owned the entire world beneath their feet. They had also worn their costumes and she realized with a sinking feeling that she really had been co-opted onto their team.

"Come on, let's go inside," said Brianna. "Let everyone check out our brand new look. They will be so jealous. By the time everyone is wearing this, we'll be on to something else."

If Annalisa thought things outside the school had been weird, they went completely off the wall once she followed the Culture Club inside. It was almost like a scene from a movie with the four girls walking down the center of the hall while other students cleared the way to let them pass unhindered. Annalisa saw admiration on many faces, jealousy on others, and pure hatred on a few. Teachers scattered through the halls were standing in their classroom doorways, smiling and nodding at the tween superheroes as they strolled through the building like they owned it.

"We'll see you at lunch," said Brittany. "Keep showing the colors, Anna. It's important that people don't forget you're one of us now. Otherwise we'd have to teach some people a lesson." She narrowed her gaze past Annalisa's shoulder. Annalisa turned to see Breezy looking at the four of them and shaking his head in disappointment.

"Bye, Anna," said Brianna. "Teammate."

"Later." Brooklyn gave her a wry smile. The triplets turned and sauntered into their classroom.

Annalisa turned, but Breezy was already gone. He must have gone to his class already. The bell rang and she realized she was going to be late. She wasn't supposed to use her powers in school, but it was that or get marked for a tardy. She flew to her locker, dumped her stuff inside it, and then flew down the hall, up a stairwell, and made it to her class just before the late bell rang. "I'm sorry," she said.

"Don't worry about it, Anna," said her math teacher. "I'm honored you're here. Have a seat."

The entire morning was one class after another of teachers fawning over her and students trying to curry favor or otherwise exploit her newfound fame. She must have taken a dozen different selfies with others and she knew that by the evening, her entire Facebook feed would be crammed full of pictures of her on other people's timelines. Being famous was something she hadn't really prepared herself for, even at a local level. She wondered how real superheroes like Mustang Sally dealt with it.

By the time lunch rolled around, she was looking for someplace to hide, and that meant the library. She snagged her lunch bag from her locker and went up to see Torvald. He was working at his computer when she poked her head into his office. "Hi, Torvald. Can I eat in here today?"

He looked up and smiled at her. "You never have to ask, Annalisa. You know my door's always open for you."

"Thanks. I won't make a mess."

"You never do. You're one of the most considerate students in this school."

She sighed. "I just feel like I screwed everything up."

"How so?"

"I busted that bank robber on Friday, and that was good, but somehow it's gotten me mixed into the Culture Club and out of the Neighborhood Watch. There was an interview and they didn't show on the news the things I actually said. Well, they did, but they changed around stuff like the order, and they edited things out."

"They took what you said out of context?"

"Yeah, that's what I've been trying to say. I never wanted to be on the Culture Club. I never wanted any of this."

"So quit."

"I can't. It's not that easy."

Torvald raised an eyebrow. "Why not? You just go to them and say *I quit, I don't want to be on your team anymore.*"

Annalisa sighed. "Have you ever tried talking to them?"

He smiled. "Yeah, I have. You're right, it probably isn't as easy as I say."

"So what do I do? My friends hate me now and think I'm a terrible person."

"You're not a terrible person, and they know that. It might take a little time, but they'll see you're still you, Annalisa. Even if you're wearing the same costume as the triplets, that doesn't mean you're a different person."

"I just wanted to do the right thing. I thought stopping a bank robbery would be a great step forward, but now I wish I'd never seen it."

"You did a good thing, though. You stopped that guy from getting away, from hurting anyone."

"But he escaped. He can change his face. He's a real supervillain."

Torvald leaned back in his chair. "And you're a real superhero."

Annalisa laughed. "Yeah, right. You think I should go catch him?"

"Isn't that your job?"

"I'm twelve. My job is to go to school. Besides, I don't know the first thing about catching supervillains. I was just lucky before."

"Maybe you can get lucky again." Torvald reached out and gently tapped Annalisa's forehead. "Or you can use this here, because you're smart as a whip, Annalisa. I bet if you really set your mind to it, you can find your bank robber again."

"You really think so?"

"I wouldn't say it if I didn't think it."

Annalisa felt like a bit of the weight of the world had been lifted off her shoulders. "Thanks, Torvald. That helped."

He smiled. "You're welcome, Annalisa. Now you'd better hurry up and eat. No matter what else happens out there, you're always welcome here in the library."

Annalisa went out to a table, opened her lunch bag, cracked open *On Parahuman Combat*, and began to read.

Chapter Fifteen

In the movies or on TV, tracking down a mysterious bank robber would have been easy. He would have left a trail of convenient clues so simple that any group of kids and their stupid dog could have followed it to his eventual capture. Unfortunately, Annalisa was discovering things weren't nearly as simple in real life.

After her lunchtime conversation with Torvald in the library, she came to a decision and did something she'd never done before: she ditched her afternoon classes and left the school grounds altogether. She'd thought about leaving her costume behind, or going home to change into something that made her feel more like herself instead of an impostor, but for what she had in mind, being associated with the Culture Club would make her job that much easier.

As soon as she sneaked out of a side door of the school, she flew straight up. People might see her if she ran away from the building, but almost nobody bothered to look in the sky. She wished she had her cape flapping behind her as she oriented herself and flew toward downtown in search of a large white building with tall windows on one side. As a local joke, people called it the Hall of Justice after its superficial resemblance to the iconic building from the cartoon. Since it held the police department along with other city offices, the nickname actually made sense.

The inside didn't look anything like police departments on TV shows. It was a long, wide hall decorated with sculptures and angled dividers bearing artwork from one of the local high schools. Display cases along the walls held glimpses of the history of Loveland, from the Native American tribes who had inhabited the area before the settlers arrived, to the pioneers who'd come seeking gold and silver in the nearby river and found a different sort of wealth in rich farmland and abundant space for ranching. Annalisa hadn't ever been inside the building before and felt very small with the tall ceiling arching overhead. The offices lined both walls, with a stairwell leading up to the second floor. She saw signs pointing out offices for various licenses, courts, and finally spotted one that said *Department of Public Safety*. That looked promising to her. She started toward it when the door opened and a pair of police officers stepped through it.

One was as tall as a tree, with skin the same color as Breezy's and hair trimmed so short it was practically just stubble. He was chuckling at something the other had said, a Hispanic woman a good foot shorter than him with a severe haircut and a sparkling smile. They jingled when they walked with all the gear on their belts. Annalisa's eyes widened and her first thought was she should fly away before she steeled herself and reminded herself why she had come to the police in the first place. "E-excuse me?"

The two officers looked down and saw her. "Can we help you?" asked the woman.

Her companion's eyes widened. "Hey, you're her. That girl from the news. The superhero. On that kids' team. What do you call them?"

The woman snapped her fingers. "The Culture Club. You're right, Bick." She bent down so she would be less threatening to Annalisa. "I'm Officer Velez, but you can call me Evie. This is Officer Bickle. What can we do for you?"

"I need to talk to the investigating officer for the bank robbery on Friday." The words came in a rush, because Annalisa had been practicing them since the first entered the building.

"You're the one who caught the suspect," said Bickle. "I saw that punch. You really cashed his check, kid."

Evie rolled her eyes. "Forgive my partner. He's a real superhero fanboy. Aren't you supposed to be in school, young lady?"

Annalisa swallowed her nervousness. "Early release today. So can I speak to the officer leading the case?"

Evie burst out laughing. "Oh, man, that's a good one. Bick, did you put her up to that?"

Tears pricked at the corners of Annalisa's eyes and she clenched her teeth to try to keep from crying.

Bickle saw her expression and judged his partner. "Hey, Evie, knock it off. I think she's serious."

"Oh sh—uh, shoot," said Evie. "You really mean it, huh?"

Annalisa nodded.

"We'll have to check to see who's been assigned as liaison to the Feds," said Bickle. "Between a federally-insured bank and parahuman involvement, the Feds are all over this one like white on rice."

"Look, kiddo, you did great work stopping that robbery, but there's not much we can do to help you here. The department is in enough hot water as it is, letting that guy walk right out the front door. There's going to be a huge investigation, you can bet your life on it." Evie shook her head.

Annalisa didn't really understand most of what she was saying, but the gist was clear enough. "I'm here to help," she said. "I'm going to help find him and bring him back to justice."

"Look, wouldn't it be better if you let us do the work of catching criminals? You'd be better off playing Minecraft or watching YouTube or whatever it is you kids do today." Evie twisted her face into what she probably thought was an amicable grin but instead looked more like a rictus of pain.

"Can I just talk to the officer?" Annalisa asked once more.

Bick scratched the stubble on his scalp. "Honestly, it's out of our hands. It's a Federal case. The PRA is involved."

Annalisa knew *PRA* meant the Parahuman Resources Agency, which was the government agency in charge of monitoring parahuman activities across the country. She wondered if any of the Just Cause heroes were involved in the case. She almost asked the two officers about it, but then decided it would be better to set aside her fangirl ways and just do her job. "Well, what about the case files you guys do have? I mean, you have to have something, right? I just want to help. I'm one of the good guys, like you."

Evie looked at Bick, and Annalisa saw that although the woman's face was still hard around her mouth, wrinkles of amusement had appeared at the corners of her eyes. "I don't know, Bick. I guess it wouldn't hurt, right?"

"Promise me this, kid. If you find him, you tell us. I know you've got parahuman powers and all, but it's our job to catch people who break the law, and we don't want you to get hurt." Bick smiled down at her. "Come on inside. If anyone asks . . ."

"We'll tell them the truth," said Evie. "You're here to follow up on your own case."

They led her inside the police station. Again, it was not what she'd expected. Instead of a big open room with dozens of desks, officers shouting into telephones, wrestling handcuffed perpetrators into holding cells, it looked more like a bland office building with cubicles. "Where is everyone?" Annalisa asked.

Bick laughed. "Working. We go out on patrol, answer calls about barking dogs or parking violations, and usually only have a bit of time here in the office to do our reports."

"You don't bring the bad guys back here?"

"No, this isn't a holding facility," said Evie. "I'll just go grab that file." She headed off toward a side room.

Bick knelt down beside Annalisa. "Listen, kid. What's your name?"

"La Capitána." Annalisa wasn't afraid of Bickle. Even though he was so large his shoulders threatened to burst apart his uniform at the seams, he didn't seem like he would hurt a fly. She suspected if he ever got angry, though, he'd be a real force with which to be reckoned.

"Captain *what?*"

"Just La Capitána. Why does it have to be Captain *something*?"

Bick smiled. "I guess it doesn't. I know I said you should call us if you find the bank robber, and I mean that. None of us want you to get hurt at all.

But if you find yourself in a position to clean his clock once more? Knock his ass out. He made our entire department look like a bunch of incompetent fools."

Annalisa's eyes widened. "Yes sir."

"*Yes sir* what?" Evie appeared around the corner of the cubicles holding a manila folder with a number stamped on it.

"I was just reminding her to be careful if she finds our escapee."

Evie glared at Bick. "That's what I thought." She turned to look at Annalisa. "All right, kid. We actually have a bit of paperwork to do so we'll be just around the corner. When we're done, you need to be done too so we can put this report away. If you need anything or have any questions, we'll be right over there." She pointed to a wide desk holding several workstations like study carrels in the school library.

Annalisa sat down in the cubicle and started paging through the report. It became apparent after a couple of minutes that she would need more time to digest all the information in it than she was likely to get with the two police officers. She glanced around to make sure nobody could see her, and then pulled out her phone and started snapping pictures of each page of the report. She could upload all the pictures to her mom's computer and then look at each one at her leisure. Or—and she smiled at the idea—maybe she could upload them on the Culture Club's computer system and look at them on the giant flat screen in their basement headquarters.

It wasn't like she was going to be hanging out with the Neighborhood Watch anytime soon.

Chapter Sixteen

"Hi, Mr. Carson," said Annalisa when he opened the door of the Arnolds' house. "Are they home?"

"Hello, Annalisa. I'm afraid not. The girls are at dance class with their mother."

"Oh. I didn't know they were dancers."

He grinned. "Yes, their mother thought they needed to be more graceful. It's all part of her vision for their brand."

Annalisa shrugged. "I guess." She started to lift off but stopped, hovering a few inches off the ground. "Do you think it would be okay if I went down to the headquarters? Even if they're not here?"

"I'm sure it's fine. They said you're part of the team, Annalisa. Come on in. You know the way. I'm working in the kitchen. Do you need a snack or anything?"

She smiled at him. "No, I'm fine. Thank you, Mr. Carson."

"You don't have to call me *Mister.*" He held the door open for her. "If you need anything, come up and get me."

Annalisa went down to the Culture Club headquarters. The lights were already on and the basement seemed cavernous without the loud, brash presence of the triplets. She appropriated a cord from the charging station the triplets had against one wall and plugged her phone into a port on the conference table. "George, can you hear me?"

"Yes, Annalisa."

Annalisa shivered at the disembodied voice echoing from multiple speakers around the headquarters. It was weird that it knew her name, even though the triplets had made a point of introducing her to it when she'd spent the night. "I'm copying some pictures from my phone onto your hard drive. Can you show them to me in order once they're uploaded?"

"Yes, Annalisa."

Her fingers danced across her phone screen as she copied the pictures into a new folder on George's desktop. Once they were all on there, she said, "Okay, let me see the first one."

An image of the first page of the report showed on the large flat screen, a little blurry because Annalisa's hand must have moved when she snapped the picture. She started reading through the report but it was a lot harder to follow than she expected. Maybe it was because whoever had written it out wasn't very good at writing. Or maybe it was because the details were so sketchy and incomplete. The report kept referring to "the Suspect" and "alleged use of parahuman abilities." She figured out early on that she was "Juvenile Parahuman A" while the rest of the Culture Club were "B, C, and D." Still, it seemed like a sanitized version of the events that had actually transpired.

She moved on to the next page, which contained more narrative. She glossed over it, wanting to get a sense of what was in the totality of the files before spending a lot of time on any one page. Plus, she didn't know how long it would take to go through all of it, and she felt it might be awkward for the triplets to return home and discover her lounging around their headquarters like she owned the place.

Then she flipped to a page with a photo identified as "Possible Suspect" and she nearly jumped out of her seat in surprise. The picture had a date and time stamp in the corner, probably a still image from the bank's security camera over the front door. It showed a man sitting in a parked car across the street from the bank, holding his phone up as if taking a picture. That wouldn't have been immediately suspicious in and of itself if the attempted robbery hadn't occurred two days later. She hadn't noticed it when the picture was mixed in with the rest of the file—it had just been one more page she'd snapped a photo of—but now, blown up on the big screen, it was as plain as day.

The man photographing the bank was Carson.

He had a bad blonde wig to hide his dark ponytail, and he had a fake blonde mustache over his lip, but there was no mistaking the chiseled features or the hawk-like nose. Annalisa immediately minimized the image and looked around, feeling a wave of guilty excitement wash over her. Had she just cracked the case? Somewhere above her head, Carson was working in the kitchen. At least, that was what he'd told her. What if he had come down the stairs while she was looking at the other parts of the file? What if he'd seen her looking at that picture?

"Hey George?" Annalisa's voice was barely above a whisper.

"Yes, Annalisa?"

"Where's Carson right now?"

"He is in the kitchen right now. Do you need to speak to him?"

"No! No no no. If he leaves the kitchen, or he's going to come downstairs, you have to warn me."

"I don't understand."

"Okay, uh, tell me if Carson leaves the kitchen."

"Yes, Annalisa."

She didn't know whether George really understood her request or not, but it would have to do for the time being. She needed to do a little more research, and unlike reading the rest of the files, she couldn't do it at home. After searching through the program files, she found the application she and the triplets had used to design their costumes. She opened it and scrolled through the dozens of files the triplets had created. They had to have one. Brooklyn had told her Carson wore the padded suit sometimes when they needed someone to train against. They must have scanned him into the costume designer at some point.

And then she found it. Shortly, a bored-looking three-dimensional render of Carson's head rotated slowly on the big screen. She selected an appropriately ugly hairstyle, colored it blonde, and placed it on the image. The mustache was harder, because the software didn't seem to have any facial hair renders in it. She wound up having to compress and reshape a hairstyle and stuck it over the image's mouth. When she finished, she sat back and took a closer look. Then she took a screen shot and compared the image of the chef in his bad wig that she'd made to the one taken outside the bank.

It wasn't a perfect match, but there was enough to it to warrant further investigation.

She didn't want to risk staying in the house any longer than she had to, now that she had identified the likely suspect. She packed up her phone and told George to delete the folder she had just created. It was dangerous to leave any data where someone might get a hold of it. She flew up the stairs and nearly ran smack into Carson.

"Oh, Annalisa, are you already leaving? I was going to bring you a snack and something to drink."

She tried to sound as nonchalant as possible. "Yeah, uh, my mom texted me. She said she needs me to come home." She gave him a wide smile. "I have chores to do."

"Well that's too bad. I like having you around, and I think it's good for the girls."

She noticed he didn't say *they* liked having her around, but she wasn't sure she could trust anything that came out of his mouth. "Yeah, uh, I like it too, but I'd better be going. Don't want to keep my mom waiting. She gets real, uh, real mad." She knew she was laying it on too thick. He was going to get suspicious.

"Do you want me to tell the girls you were by?" He noticed something on one of his hands and wiped it against his apron, which was when Annalisa realized he was wearing an apron. It was hard for her to believe he was the robber, but then she decided he had the perfect cover. Who would believe a parahuman bank robber was the butler for a trio of would-be superheroes?

Annalisa would. "No, that's okay. I'll text them on my way home. So, uh, bye!" She rushed out the door faster than she knew she should have, but seeing the image of Carson in the police file had freaked her out more than she expected once confronted by him. Before he could say anything, she was airborne and heading in the general direction of home.

After a few minutes in the sky, she had calmed down enough to feel like she could handle her phone without dropping it a hundred feet to the ground. She knew she was supposed to call the police. Officers Bickle and Velez had been firm on that direction. But somehow, she couldn't make her fingers dial those three simple numbers that would bring the police in droves. She had stopped the robbery the first time, and it was the police who had let the suspect escape. Now she had found him again. Why shouldn't she be the one to bring him back in?

Except this time, she would make sure she had some help. Proper help. Help the media couldn't edit out.

She texted Breezy.

Chapter Seventeen

"What's up, Capitána?" Breezy flew up to meet her atop the building under construction where Annalisa had first found the armored truck guards. It was late enough in the afternoon that work on the site was mostly wound down and those few workers remaining were more interested in finishing their current jobs so they could go to the bar than they were in looking up at the young superheroes. Breezy landed beside her, his winds making her hair flutter around her face.

"Is everyone still mad at me?" Annalisa stood near the edge of the rooftop, staring out at what she would always think of as *her city*.

Breezy moved to stand beside her. His cape hung on folds around him like the sky blue robes of a monk. "'S only been a couple days, Annalisa. Ain't enough time yet for them to not be so butt hurt 'bout it."

"How about you?"

He shrugged. "I guess I ain't as smart as them, because I don't see the big deal."

Annalisa smiled at him. "Thanks, Breezy. You're a good friend."

"They're all good friends. They just ain't as chill about it as me. So what's up?"

"I think I found the guy who tried to rob that bank, and then escaped."

"Who is it?"

Annalisa told him about the picture she'd seen in the police file and how it looked like the Arnolds' butler Carson. "Although I don't know if he's actually a butler. He just cooks and helps them train and drives them around." She paused, thinking. "Drives them around. Hmmm."

"What is it?"

"Well, I was just thinking. Sometimes he drives them and sometimes their mom does. Maybe we should find out if he was there on the day of the robbery. Or on the date of that picture." She waved her phone.

"They're your friends," said Breezy. He raised his fingers and made the dust atop the roof dance and swirl.

Annalisa shook her head. "They're not my friends. I don't even think they think they are. They just want to use me to be more famous."

"So what you gonna do, Annalisa? And what you need from me?"

"I'm going to have to go back and talk to them. Find out what they know. And I need to find out more about Carson. That's what I need from you. Go talk to Wheels. Tell her anything you have to, but I need her help. She's got those cameras, right? Maybe she can look at her recordings and find something. And I need Rascal too, with his followers. Breezy . . . I need all you guys. You're my team, not the Culture Club. Not ever."

"I know what I'll tell them. You're just workin' undercover, like on TV."

"You think that'll work?"

"Yeah."

"Thanks, Breezy. You're the best."

He grinned. "I'm gonna remember you said that next time we ain't gettin' on so good." He raised his fingers to his lips, kissed them, and waved. "I'm out." His cape inflated and he flew away, leaving Annalisa behind to contemplate how to proceed with her investigation.

She knew she needed to talk to the triplets, but wasn't sure how to manage it. Together, it was impossible to get a word in edgewise around them, and they fed off each other like fires burning toward each other to create a gigantic inferno. And they were never apart, so talking to just one of them was a practical impossibility.

Maybe through texting? She doubted they consulted each other before replying to texts. Nobody would do that, right? Not even the triplets.

But what to ask? She couldn't just ask "Hey, was Carson with you the day of the robbery?" without raising suspicions.

Maybe the better question was why she was worried about raising suspicions at all. She replayed the entire robbery in her mind while sitting at the edge of the rooftop, kicking her feet over the edge and twisting her fingers in her hair.

Then she had it. Brittany had said *You're not supposed to be here.* That wasn't right. What was it Brittany had expected that Annalisa had interrupted?

A robbery, of course.

"She knew." Annalisa stood, clenching her fists. "She knew it was going to happen!"

She launched herself into the sky, flying higher and faster than she'd ever dared to before. Anger coursed through her. She'd missed it completely. The triplets had overwhelmed her with all their attention and fancy headquarters and matching uniforms, but at the end of the day, they had known the bank was going to be robbed and they were there to stop it. When Annalisa had stumbled upon it, they'd been surprised and had to improvise to deal with her.

If they'd known about the robbery, they had to know about Carson. They had to have planned it with him. Annalisa had a mind to go confront them, to make them confess, but she knew she couldn't. Not by herself. She hurtled through the sky, gritting her teeth in frustration. It felt like there was nothing she could do. She spotted a familiar stretch of dirt walled in by crushed cars with the innocuous white blotch of a Winnebago parked in one corner and her anger grew much more acute. How *dare* they kick her out? She was their friend!

She dropped to the ground like a missile on final approach. When she twisted down to land feet first, the nearby stacks of cars rattled with the impact, and dirt flew outward to put her at the center of a small, Annalisa-sized crater. She didn't care. She needed to break something, to hit something. A bumper found its way into her hands and she squeezed it, listening to the sound of overstressed metal. She bent it under her arm until she'd twisted it into an unrecognizable shape, then flung it aside.

Still angry, she wrenched a wheel off a wreck, then tore the hub out from the tire and threw it as hard as she could into another stack. The wheel embedded itself in a rusted car door and stuck there. She grasped the inside edge of the tire and pulled, trying to tear it apart. Her shoulders and back ached with the effort and she grew angrier, as if it were the triplets' fault. Rubber parted ways suddenly, steel cables snapping like overtightened guitar strings. Annalisa was left holding two pieces of ripped tire and a suddenly increasing rank odor. She threw them away.

Her temper still flared like Hothead's hair. She punched a wrecked van, denting the sheet metal of the side. It made her knuckles sting—the first time she'd felt anything in her tantrum. She punched it again, reveling in the slight pain, knowing she was pushing herself past her limits and not caring. *Wham!* She punched it once more and her fist scraped through jagged metal. It hurt enough to make her yelp. She pulled back in reflex and sharp edges poked her all around her wrist. Somehow the metal had flexed when her fist went through it and she was trapped. No matter how she twisted her wrist around, she couldn't find an angle to pull herself free without raw edges threatening to cut through her natural toughness.

She sniffled and realized tears were running down her cheeks. "Dang it," she whispered. "You dumbass."

"No argument here," said a voice behind her.

Annalisa looked over her shoulder to see Wheels sitting in her chair, leaning on one arm and resting her chin on her upraised hand. Her face grew hot and she quickly wiped her eyes with her free hand. "What are you doing here?"

"I live here. I should be asking you that, except I see you're busy tearing apart my dad's scrap yard."

"I'm not . . . I mean, yeah, okay, I was. I'm sorry."

"Why are you here, Annalisa?"

"I'm stuck."

A wry grin tugged at one corner of Wheels' mouth. "I can see that, dumbass. I mean why are you here at all?"

"I was mad. I got burned by the Culture Club. I never should have trusted them and now I don't know what to do."

"Yeah, Breezy just called me like five minutes before I saw you doing your best Bombshell impression. He said you needed us."

"I do need you. I need all of you guys. You're my friends. The triplets, they're just mean. I never wanted to be part of their group. I already have a team, Aighleigh. Yours. Ours. The Neighborhood Watch."

Wheels smiled. "I wonder if Just Cause ever goes through these kinds of fights."

Annalisa's return smile was tinged with pain. "I don't know, but do you think maybe you could cut me free? I know you've got tools and stuff in your kit."

Wheels didn't move, and her smile disappeared. "First I want to hear you say it. Say you're sorry."

"Wheels . . . Aighleigh, I'm so sorry. I'm a jerk and an ass. I never meant to hurt any of you. I love you guys." Annalisa wiped her eyes again.

Wheels rolled over, rummaging through a side compartment. "I accept your apology. I don't know if I could have stayed mad at you that long anyway. Without you, we're just a bunch of kids sitting around in a Winnebago. Maybe I'm the brains of the team, but you're the heart."

"Who said you were the brains?"

Wheels held up a device. "This microlaser cutting torch says it."

Annalisa had to concede the point.

Chapter Eighteen

"Uh-uh. No way. She had her chance." Hothead shook his head, sparks dancing across his hairline. "And she threw us under the bus."

"Why you bein' such a jerk, Cole?" asked Breezy. He'd sat and watched as Wheels cut Annalisa's hand free of the sheet metal and then brought some ice to help soothe the reddening of her skin from the laser torch. "She came back to apologize. You can't take it like a man?"

"Say that to my face, Bryson." Hothead pointed at Breezy. "You're just taking her side because you *like* her."

Annalisa gasped. She wondered if it was true, but she had no time to consider it in depth, for Breezy jumped to his feet and got all up in Hothead's face.

"You want I should say it to your face? How 'bout now? 'Cause if anyone here's bein' a sorry jerk, it's you."

Hothead's hair lit up like a torch and he pushed Breezy away. "Get off!"

Breezy tripped on his cape and fell back against Wheels. "Stop it, you guys!" she yelled. "This isn't how we're supposed to act! You're going to set our headquarters on fire."

Breezy jumped back up, spoiling for a fight. A sudden, swirling wind filled the Winnebago, sending papers and bottlecaps flying in every direction.

Wheels sighed and touched a switch on the arm of her chair. Something made a sharp *pop* noise. Breezy twitched for a moment and the gum fell out of his mouth, then he collapsed in a heap on the floor. Two coiled wires stretched from darts in his back to Wheels' chair. Annalisa ran to kneel beside him. "Breezy!"

Hothead started to laugh raucously at Breezy's plight, but with a *whoosh*, a jet of white foam blasted him in the face, knocking him over and leaving his head a sodden mess.

Rascal lowered the fire extinguisher and shrugged. "He had it coming."

Wheels yanked on the ends of her wheelchair taser, pulling them free so they wouldn't be in her way. "If you two idiots are done measuring your boy-parts, can we get back to the reason we're all here in the first place?"

Breezy sat up and shook his head as if clearing cobwebs from it. "Man, that sucked."

Hothead coughed and sent bits of foam flying. "I mean, yeah."

Annalisa stood. "You guys, if anyone here was a jerk, it was me. I'm sorry I got pulled into the Culture Club's world. You're my team, my friends, and this is where I belong. Can you forgive me?"

Breezy picked up the gum he'd lost when he was shocked, looked at it sadly, and tossed it into the trash. "That was a fresh piece, too. Yeah, I forgive you, Annalisa."

"Oh Captain, my Captain," said Wheels. "Me too."

Rascal smirked at her. "I wasn't ever really down with her leaving in the first place. She was always one of us."

"Guess that leaves you, Cole," said Annalisa. She didn't have a towel handy, so she offered him her cape to wipe off his face. He looked at it in surprise. She shrugged. "I can always wash it. Or make a new one. It's just a piece of cloth."

He waved her away. "No. It means more than that to you."

"And she just offered it to you to wipe crud off your face," said Wheels. "That's kind of a big deal."

Hothead nodded. "Yeah, I get it. Can we just all agree that we were all wrong and get on with things?"

Annalisa held her hand out to Hothead. He looked at it for a moment like she had cooties, but then he took it and she pulled him to his feet. "Sorry, Cole."

"It's okay." Wheels tossed a rag to him and he wiped off his face the best he could. "So what's our next move?"

Annalisa told them all about her suspicions around Carson. "I think it's him," she said in conclusion. "It makes perfect sense, and the Culture Club is in on it."

"You think they set it all up? The robbery?" asked Rascal.

"Yeah, I do. Brittany said I wasn't supposed to be there. They had planned it all out with Carson, but they hadn't expected me to show up."

"And that's why they made you join up with them," said Hothead. "That's how they covered it up."

"We got to stop them," said Breezy.

"Stop them from doing what?" asked Wheels.

"Whatever they gonna do next."

"We don't know what they're going to do next," said Wheels. "But we can start working on that. And maybe if we get lucky with our surveillance records, we can catch something crucial the police might have missed."

"I don't think they were ever looking at the Culture Club as suspects," said Annalisa. "And why would they? They're superheroes. They're famous."

"They're *locally* famous," said Wheels. "Stopping the bank robbery got them more national fame. It's what they want. What we need to do is follow them. Stay close. Catch them in a mistake." She looked at Annalisa. "You're going to have to go undercover."

Annalisa blinked in surprise. "What do you mean?"

"They still think you're in their group, right?"

"As far as I know, yeah."

"Then until they kick you out, you should keep hanging around them. Either they'll have to kick you to the curb because they don't want you to find out the truth, or they'll have to bring you into the secret. Either way, we'll have a better idea of what they're going to do next."

"That would keep me closer to Carson," said Annalisa. "I'd be more likely to catch him in a mistake too. See him use his powers and then we'd know for sure."

"But what do we do then? Call the cops? They're not going to believe a bunch of kids, even if we do have parahuman powers," said Hothead.

"They will if we have evidence," said Rascal. "Video. Pictures. Recordings. Eyewitness stuff. It's media power. They got it right now. We can turn that against them. People love to see their heroes fall."

Over the next couple of hours, Annalisa and the others watched Wheels and Rascal work their magic, one with homegrown surveillance technology and the other with an ever-growing base of social media followers. Even though she didn't understand half of what they were doing, there was something about watching experts in their fields work which was enjoyable nevertheless.

Wheels flew three of her tiny drones to the Arnolds' house. Careful navigation through the close quarters of tree branches allowed her to park them in trees around the residence where they could train their cameras upon the exits, hopefully without being spotted.

Rascal sent out tweets and Instagrams and Tumblrs, sharing the picture from the police file along with a message to his followers. Annalisa read it aloud and everyone laughed. "*Yoooo! Any1 see this dood reply. Post a pic if u can.*"

Rascal grinned. "That'll get people looking for him. If Wheels sees him leave, I can alert my followers. They'll find him."

"Probably you'll say somethin' like *yoooo dude is on the move.*" Breezy chuckled.

"Probably I will."

"So what happens now?" Annalisa asked.

"We wait," said Wheels. "Sooner or later my drones will see something, or one of Rascal's followers. Then we have some information to go on and we can act."

"What do you want to do until then?" The foam had dried in Hothead's hair, giving it a spiky appearance. Annalisa wondered what would happen if he flamed on before taking his next shower. Would the extinguisher chemicals keep it from happening or would he overcome them?

Breezy opened the refrigerator. "Mexican Cokes, yo." He passed out bottles. "What would the Culture Club be doing right now if they was us?"

Annalisa shrugged. "Probably training in their fancy headquarters. Or designing new costumes to wear." She grimaced. "I'm going to have to wear that terrible one they made for me until they change it up again."

Wheels giggled. "It looks like someone spilled a paint can full of pixels over you."

The others laughed. Annalisa made a goofy face and Hothead sprayed Coke out his nose. "Oh dang it. That stings." He rubbed his nose.

The amusement of her friends made Annalisa feel like she was back where she belonged. Her friends didn't have fancy high-tech gadgets or a shiny headquarters or a butler, but they did have each other and that was better than the triplets, who were basically a single person when one got right down to considering it. She wondered if maybe they were lonely and that was why they acted the way they did to other people. She supposed if she had parents like theirs, she might be a little screwed up in the head too.

Rascal raised his phone to take a picture, then frowned and swiped at his screen. Once he did so, all trace of jocularity vanished from his face.

"What is it, Rascal?" asked Wheels.

He turned his phone around to show them. "I just got an Instagram. One of my followers. She just asked *is this him?*"

On the screen was a clear image of Carson, or a man who looked very much like him. He was standing on a street corner outside of a coffee shop, a large paper cup clutched in one hand while the other was held up in mid-conversational gesture. Even on the small phone screen, Annalisa was fairly certain it was indeed Carson, right down to the dark stubble and man-ponytail. If it wasn't him, it was someone who looked enough like him to be a twin, just like the man he was speaking to looked just like . . .

"Hey, isn't that Torvald?" asked Hothead, his itchy Coke nose forgotten.

Anger raced through Annalisa. What was Carson doing? Torvald was *hers*. The librarian was her only real adult friend, and she wasn't about to let some supervillain take him away! "Where is this?" she growled. "The picture. Where was it taken? How old is it?"

Rascal stared at her, wide-eyed, before checking the picture's location data and timestamp. "Corner of West 8th and Hennesey Road. *Bower's Coffee*. And that's only about a minute before I got the picture. He's—"

But Annalisa didn't hear what Rascal had started to say. She rushed out the door of the headquarters.

"Annalisa? Capitána?" called Wheels after her, but Annalisa didn't wait. The longer she tarried, the more chance she had of missing them altogether.

She threw herself into the sky and headed east as fast as she could.

Chapter Nineteen

Annalisa felt like a missile acquiring her target. Carson was still standing with Torvald next to Bower's Coffee. Only a couple of minutes could have passed since Rascal's follower sent him the notification. At first, Annalisa had considered confronting Carson in the Arnold household, but that would have been awkward, and could even have grown ugly if the triplets had discovered her real purpose for being there. Next, she'd thought about maybe landing beside him and trying to have a mature, grown-up conversation, telling herself she was protecting Torvald from a very dangerous man, but the closer she got to the coffee shop, the less it seemed like it would end on any kind of good note. Talking to grownups was hard enough since they always had the power of authority and age working in their favor. She had to break that power if she was going to get any useful information out of Carson.

She came in low and fast, zig-zagging around pedestrians, who shouted in surprise as she passed. Torvald spotted her. His eyes widened and coffee splattered around the edges of his cup. Before he could issue so much as a "Hey!" Annalisa grabbed hold of Carson and shot straight up into the air.

Carson's girly shriek was so satisfactory Annalisa almost dropped him in the hope of hearing it again. His coffee went flying as he kicked at the air. Torvald's plaintive cry echoed after her but Annalisa ignored it as she gained speed and altitude. Holding the struggling Carson under his arms was a lot like picking up a squirming puppy, only without the face-licking. Still, he needed to be told . . . "You better stop kicking or I'm going to drop you, and neither of us want that, Carson."

"A-a-annalisa?" He tensed up but stopped struggling, which made it much easier to carry him. She wouldn't have dropped him, because that was what supervillains did, not heroes.

"Just hold still. This'll all be over soon." She headed toward the top of the building under construction.

"What are you d-doing? Oh God, I hate heights . . ."

"Don't you dare puke," said Annalisa. She set him on a steel crossbeam next to a vertical girder.

He grabbed onto the girder with white-knuckled desperation. Tears streamed down his cheeks as he tried to hold onto everything at once.

"Why? Why did you do this?" It was such a marked change from the confident, handsome chef that Annalisa had no problem believing this was a supervillain who could change his face.

"I'll ask the questions." Annalisa tried to put a forceful tone into her voice. This was how she had chosen to level the playing field. Carson had no adult authority up at the top of the building, and she expected answers. "First of all, why were you talking to Torvald?"

"Why . . . Annalisa, he's my husband. Of course I'm going to t-talk to him."

Annalisa paused. She'd expected something far more sinister, like they were conspiring together about their next devious robbery. "How come I never saw you together before?"

Carson's sigh was full of the same kind of exasperation Annalisa heard from her mom when she'd had about enough of a middle schooler's attitude. "Because he has his job, and I have mine, and you're not around us twenty-four hours a day."

"No, but the triplets are. I mean . . . aren't they?"

"I'm not a slave, Annalisa. I get two days off a week, and I don't sleep at the Arnolds' house. Tor and I have a nice little condo on the west side. I cook and clean, and he reads books to me while I do. It's lovely." He glanced down and turned a little green beneath his stubble. "Now will you p-please put me back on the ground?"

"Not so fast, Carson. I saw you, in the police file. You were watching the bank before the robbery. You changed your face!"

"I what? What are you talking about?"

Annalisa pulled out her phone. She flew around the girder until she was facing him, hovering in midair. She showed him the picture she'd taken of the police file. "There. See?"

At first Carson only glanced at the phone, and then looked again, his eyebrows coming together as he studied it. "Annalisa, that's not me. I've never worn a mustache, and I wouldn't be caught dead in that hairdo. That's not even my car."

"Of course it's you! You're the guy, the one who robbed the bank. I knocked you out." She raised a fist. "And I'll do it again if you don't tell me the truth."

"I can see why you'd think it's me. Whoever it is looks a lot like me. I don't know why, but I swear it's not me, and I can prove it. Please, Annalisa. Hear me out. Just set me on solid ground first. P-please."

The fear in his voice was genuine, at least. Annalisa could see his white knuckles as he gripped the girder, the quivering in his arm muscles. "All right, but no funny business. I can fly faster than you can run, and you already know I'm strong enough to knock you out."

"Only because I saw the video of you knocking that guy out. I p-promise it wasn't me. Oh God, please don't drop me."

Annalisa flew in behind Carson and wrapped her arms around his chest under his arms. "I won't drop you. Uh, Carson, you have to let go."

"N-no!"

"Carson!"

"Sorry. Oh, geez." Carson's legs buckled and he became dead weight in Annalisa's arms.

She realized he had fainted and carefully flew him across the construction to a completed floor in the building. She set him down against a wall and shook him, gently enough that she wouldn't hurt him with her parahuman strength. "Carson, wake up. You're safe now. You're on a floor." She shook him again and he stirred.

"A floor," he mumbled. He looked around slowly, like a turtle waking up, and saw she was telling the truth. "Annalisa. I'm sorry. I got dizzy for a second."

"You fainted."

He snorted. "Nonsense. The height must have gotten to me."

Annalisa crossed her arms. "You said you were going to prove that you weren't the bank robber. So, prove it."

He sighed. "I'm probably going to be in terrible trouble for this." He reached into his back pocket.

Annalisa stiffened and clenched her fists. "Hey, I said no funny business."

He held up his other hand. "It's okay, I'm just taking out my ID. I'm not who you think I am. I mean, I'm still me." He held up a badge with his picture and identification attached to it. "Special Agent Carson Howe, Parahuman Resources Agency."

"The PRA? You're with the PRA?"

"Both of us are. Tor and I."

"What are you doing here, though?"

Carson put away his badge. "We're on a long-term assignment. We've been here for the past five years."

"Why here?"

"What do you know about parahuman population statistics, Annalisa?"

Annalisa shrugged. "Nothing, I guess."

"Current figures estimate the incidence of parahuman abilities occur about once for every two to three million people. That means thousands of them around world, but statistically unlikely except in the largest population centers. This state should only have two or three naturally-occurring parahumans within its population base." Carson held up eight fingers. "And yet, there are eight of you in this tiny little town, all born within three weeks of each other. That's way beyond normal statistical variances. Do you understand what that means?"

"I guess it's kind of weird?" Annalisa was fascinated in spite of her suspicions. Whether he intended to or not, Carson was playing right to her strongest interests in all things parahuman.

"It's not just *kind of* weird. It's *extremely weird.* Tor and I came here to monitor the eight of you and try to figure out how you came to exist."

"What do you mean, how I came to exist? I've been to health class if that's what you mean."

"That's not what I mean. Annalisa . . . You're not a parahuman. None of your friends are. Nor are the triplets."

Annalisa sat down in shock. "What do you m-mean? Of course we are. Aren't we?"

"None of you have the genetic markers for parahumans. We've tested all of you as we've had the opportunity to do so. Likewise for your parents. All of your Musashi tests are negative. None of you should have abilities. And yet, all of you do. We can't explain that, which is why the PRA has Tor and I here to monitor you and your friends. We're . . . concerned that you may be the result of an illegal experiment, and if that's the case, we need to make sure nobody comes around to collect the results of the experiment."

"You mean kidnap us? I'd like to see someone try it." Annalisa punched her fist into her open palm.

"I wouldn't. If someone was able to give you abilities, they might be able to take them away. And we don't want anything to happen to you or your friends." Carson smiled. "Even though they can be trying at times, I must admit I've grown rather fond of the triplets, and I know Tor has taken a special liking to you and your friends. Speaking of which, I really ought to call him and tell him I'm all right. Do you mind?"

"No, I guess not." Annalisa watched as Carson took out his phone and spoke into it briefly. She couldn't quite hear what he said, and felt it would be rude to move closer to listen better, but he mostly seemed to be calming Tor, and ended the conversation with an *I love you too.* "Why do you think the bank robber used your face?"

"Well, I do chauffeur the triplets around from time to time when their mom and dad are working. That might put my face above suspicion if someone recognizes it, like you did."

"Well, whoever it is did a good job. I recognized it as you right away, even with that bad mustache and hair. It's like they already knew what you looked like and then made you look dumb intentionally."

Carson rubbed his jaw. "Shapeshifters need to spend time studying their subjects. It's an uncommon ability and that has so far been a prerequisite for it. It's possible this is a new shapeshifter who can learn new subjects instantaneously, but until I see evidence of it, I'm going to operate on the theory this particular shapeshifter has to study."

"How much studying? I mean, can they just look at pictures or do they need to be around you or what?"

"It's hard to say. It might not be an unreasonable assumption that it's someone who's seen me before and who's had time to really look at me. Maybe it's someone from one of my days off. Someplace I go fairly regularly, like the gym or the coffee shop."

An idea occurred to Annalisa. "Or maybe it's something else. Will you and Torvald come to our headquarters? This way I don't have to tell the same story twice, and it's one you all need to hear."

"Sure, I'd love to meet the rest of the Neighborhood Watch." Carson grinned. "After all, you're the Just Cause heroes of the future."

Annalisa felt her cheeks get hot and she lifted off the floor, floating in an expression of pride. "Do you want me to fly you back down?"

Carson's smile became pained. "I'll take the stairs, thanks."

Chapter Twenty

Annalisa would have paced if she'd had the room, but with Torvald and Carson inside the Winnebago along with the rest of the Neighborhood Watch, it was almost too crowded for her to move at all. "So here's the thing. I'm pretty sure the triplets knew all about the robbery attempt before it happened."

"Why do you say that, Annalisa?" Torvald asked.

She smiled at him. It was like he was coaching her. She wondered if that was what he'd been doing all the time he'd been giving her books to read on parahumans. Maybe in his own way, he was encouraging her to become the superhero she'd always dreamed of becoming. "When Brittany saw me at the robbery, before it started, she said *what are you doing here?* You know, like she wasn't expecting me to be there at all."

"Why would she expect you?" Hothead yawned.

"No, you're not thinking it through, Cole." Wheels looked up from the gadget she was assembling on her workbench. "It's the timing of the thing. They were in the same place as the robbery, and they weren't expecting to see anyone else. That's because they were going to stop the robbery themselves."

"Well, how were they gonna do it if they didn't know it was . . ." Breezy stopped and his eyes widened as he figured it out. "They *did* know! That's why they were there, right?"

Annalisa pointed at him and winked. "Right. They were in on it. I bet they've been in on a lot of the things where they've been the heroes of the moment. Nobody is in the right place and the right time that much without getting help."

"So where were you during the robbery, Carson?" Rascal was amusing himself by using his power to stick a piece of his armor to himself and then dropping it and catching it. The others stared at him and he shrugged. "What? I have to ask. It's what TV cops would do."

"It's also what real cops would do, Rascal," said Carson. "I was in the Arnolds' house, straightening up before getting ready to start dinner. My days off are Monday and Tuesday." He raised a hand to forestall more questions. "And unfortunately, no, I can't prove it."

"Hey, check this out," said Wheels. Everyone turned to look. "You know how I've been setting up our own surveillance camera network? I had one nearby the bank and I just checked the feed from the day before the robbery and look!" She pointed at one of the TVs and a grainy image appeared on it of a dark blob that might have been a car on a street. "Hang on, let me clean that up." She clicked her mouse around the screen, operating filters and layers. The image resolved into a dark car with the mustachioed fake-Carson driving it.

"That's not my car," he said. "I've got a white Toyota. I don't even know what that is."

"It's an Audi A7," said Hothead. "That's a heck of a nice car for a bank robber to drive."

"Maybe he needed it for a quick getaway?" asked Rascal.

Annalisa shook her head. "He wasn't going to use the car in the robbery at all. He was going to use the armored truck. What's the matter, Carson?" She noticed Carson's face had gone pale and he was leaning against the wall of the headquarters. "You gonna be sick?"

He grimaced as if there were a bad taste in his mouth. "No, but I just realized whose car that is."

"Well, don't keep us all in suspense." Wheels crossed her arms. "We've got a city to save."

"That's Ben Arnold's company car," said Carson.

"Who?" asked Breezy.

"Oh my gosh!" cried Annalisa. "Mr. Arnold is the triplets' dad!"

"It can't be him," said Torvald. "We've tested his DNA. He's not a Musashi carrier."

"Why can't it be him?" asked Annalisa. "Carson said none of us are. We've all got powers. So do the triplets. Why can't he have them too?"

"I . . . I don't actually know," said Torvald. "Help me out here, babe."

Carson shrugged. "Maybe he does. We can try testing him again. I'll have ample opportunity once my days off are over. All I have to do is get hold of his water glass and we can run a quick swab test on it."

"I'll do it," said Annalisa. "Right now they don't suspect me. I can hang out with them and I'll take one when I have a chance."

"I've got a drone that can carry cargo as heavy as a water glass," said Wheels. "I'll park it in the trees outside. Annalisa won't even have to sneak away to get it to you. All she has to do is put it outside." She spun a screwdriver slowly through her fingers, watching it twist as she spoke. "It kind of makes sense if he's the robber, though. He's the one always covering them in the news. They wouldn't be famous without him. They'd be like us. Just hoping for a chance to do something."

"When did you test his DNA?" asked Rascal. "Maybe he got powers since then."

Torvald shook his head. "That's not how parahuman powers work."

Annalisa turned to Carson. "But you said that none of us have the Musashi gene either, and we have powers. So how did we get ours? Maybe he got his the same way."

Carson sighed. "I don't know. I don't have any answers, Annalisa. I wish I did. This was already complicated before bringing a possible supervillain into this."

Breezy sat up suddenly. "Oooh, I got an idea! What if their pops really don't have the DNA thing, but now this shapeshifter dude is pretending to be their pops? Like, he replaced him."

Carson looked at Torvald, who grinned back. "That's a really good idea, Breezy. We're going to have to get into the PRA database and see what we can find out about known and suspected shapeshifter parahumans. That would be a good place to start."

Torvald said, "I'm pretty sure we did our initial test three years ago, when all your powers first manifested and the PRA assigned us to investigate. He could have been replaced since then."

"Wouldn't the triplets know?" asked Hothead. "I mean, I'm pretty sure I'd know if someone else disguised himself as my dad. Maybe I'd get to have ice cream a little more often."

"Something like that doesn't just happen without anyone's knowledge," Torvald said. "It's a good bet that if Breezy's theory turns out to be accurate, Mrs. Arnold is in on it."

Carson's fingers danced across his tablet. "Wheels, do you have a cord so I can connect this to your system? I'd like to be able to show this to all of you."

Wheels snickered. "Um, I've been following along since you first started working." She touched some keys on her wireless keyboard and the screen image of Carson's tablet appeared on one of the televisions on the wall. "You need to improve your wifi security."

Carson's mouth hung open in surprise for a moment and then snapped shut. Torvald burst out laughing. "I told you, these kids put us to shame in so many ways." The librarian reached out to squeeze his husband's arm. "Just run with it, babe."

Carson cleared his throat. His face was red enough that Annalisa wondered if he was about to burst into flames like Hothead. "Ahem. As I was saying. We currently have twelve known and four more suspected shapeshifter parahumans in the PRA database. That's worldwide, by the way. Shapeshifting is an uncommon ability. Of those sixteen, we can cross eleven off the list thanks to current information on their locations. That leaves us with five unknowns."

Torvald pointed at the screen. "This guy is wanted by the feds in connection with the Chessboard Industries fiasco a few years back. I just can't picture him getting involved in a small-town bank robbery scheme."

"People can fall a long way," said Carson. "But yeah, I kind of think you're right here. Let's not discount him entirely, but maybe place him at the bottom of the list. These three are Chinese, and we don't have any firm information on them at all."

"So what about this guy here?" Annalisa pointed to the last one on the list. "*Le Masque*. Is that French?"

Carson opened the file on the name. "Gérard Chrétien. Small-time French parahuman criminal. Last known sighting in February of 2015. Suspected to have been involved in some shady doings in Paris during the early 2010s. Two of his known associates were found dead and burned in a van. A third victim was never identified but French authorities suspect it was him. Without any way to clearly identify the victim and no next of kin to claim it, the victim was buried in a pauper's grave."

"Hey, you know who else was in Paris that February?" asked Wheels. She opened a magazine article on Fashion Week 2015 on an adjoining screen. The attached picture featured a model showing off a bodysuit-themed outfit from BASH Designs. "Barb Arnold herself, along with her plus one."

"I remember that," said Carson. "It was right after I started working for the Arnolds. Maybe only a week. I'd barely had the chance to get to know either of the parents, between her business trip and his long hours for the news."

"You think maybe the real Arnold died in Paris and Chrétien took his place?" asked Torvald. "Surely Mrs. Arnold would have seen through that. And the triplets, too."

"Unless she was in on it," said Rascal. "Maybe she cooked it up with the French guy. Maybe they were having an affair or something." Everyone looked at him. "I mean, he's French, right? I've seen TV shows."

"It's the best lead we have right now," said Carson. "I think we'll start there. Annalisa, you see about getting that DNA sample for us. I'll contact headquarters and see if they can have French authorities exhume the body and try to withdraw a genetic sample for us."

"What good will that do if you don't have Le Masque's info on file?" asked Annalisa.

"They don't have to have it," said Wheels. "They have the real Mr. Arnold's. If it's his DNA, then we know he got replaced. Just like if your sample turns out not to match his."

Annalisa nodded. "Got it. Anyone else have any questions?"

"Give me a minute, I'll think of one," said Rascal.

"I'm ignoring you." Annalisa nodded at Wheels. "Call it, Wheels."

Wheels nodded back. "Neighborhood Watch, let's roll!"

Chapter Twenty-One

"I was thinking about superhero names," said Annalisa over slices of pizza in the Arnolds' kitchen. "I mean, you guys just use your first names, and I guess that's okay, but it's not really building a brand, right?"

"Of course it's building a brand," said Brianna. "Mom knows all about that kind of stuff. That's what she's all about with BASH Designs. That's a brand."

"No, that's not what I mean." Annalisa picked a sausage piece off her slice and ate it by itself. "Using just your names is kind of, you know, old school. And when you guys are always changing your costumes, people aren't going to identify you as a brand. Look at Mustang Sally. She's had pretty much the exact same look since she was a kid in the Hero Academy. And the same name. That makes her easy for people to remember."

"Are you saying people aren't going to remember us?" Brittany set down her pizza and crossed her arms. "Because you're wrong. We're triplets. People will remember that."

"But they won't remember your names, because they're just names. They don't *mean* anything. Lots of girls are named Brittany or Brianna or Brooklyn. They don't tell anything about your powers. And my name doesn't even fit in with yours. Three Bs and an A? That sounds like a report card."

Brooklyn snorted. "Better than I got last semester."

"I think you're just being stupid," said Brittany, in a tone that brooked no argument. "We're a brand. The parahuman triplets. We're the only ones in the world. We could call ourselves Huey, Dewey, and Louie, and people would still remember us. Isn't that right, Daddy?"

Everyone turned to look at Ben Arnold where he sat at one end of the table, two slices of pizza and a half-eaten piece of garlic bread on his plate. He'd been sitting and listening to the conversation without interjecting much of his own opinion. Annalisa wondered if he was studying her so he might be able to copy her someday, which made her very uncomfortable. She couldn't manage much more than to glance in his direction occasionally. "Oh, I don't know, girls. I think Annalisa is making a valid point about your super-identities. Code-names and iconic words stand out more in media and popular culture than do regular names. Most people don't know who Molly Berryfield is, but anyone who's listened to rock music the past ten years has heard of her band Yojimbo. Maybe you girls should think about some superhero-type names. I mean, the Culture Club name for the team is good. It has a lot of recognition in social media."

"You want us to come up with superhero names? How hard can that be?" asked Brianna. "Annalisa did it."

Annalisa was about to say something but she saw movement through the window over Ben Arnold's shoulder and she nearly dropped her pizza because of it. Rascal's head popped down from above the window to peek inside. He must have been using his clinging ability to stick to the wall over the window. He saw Annalisa staring at him and gave her a frantic wave. Then he made a drinking-from-a-bottle motion and then ducked back out of sight overhead once more.

Annalisa cleared her throat. "I see you finished your beer, Mr. Arnold. Can I get you another one?" She said it too loud and too fast and she knew it. Before he could reply, she grabbed his bottle.

Arnold didn't seem to notice her awkwardness. "That's all right, Anna. One of the girls can get me one. Brooklyn . . ."

"No, it's no trouble at all. I'll be right back." Annalisa dashed into the kitchen, hoping none of the triplets followed her.

Rascal poked his head down to the kitchen window as she pulled it open. "Hurry up!"

Annalisa had to poke her finger through the screen and break a slit into it big enough to push the bottle through. "Hurry up yourself, and don't drop it!" she whispered back at him. He stuck the bottle to his arm and crawled back up out of sight, just as she slammed the window shut.

"What are you doing?"

Annalisa squeaked and turned to see Brooklyn regarding her with an eyebrow raised and her arms folded. "I, uh, caught a spider. A big one. I put it outside."

Brooklyn grimaced. "Ew. You didn't just step on it?"

"Ew. Then I'd have spider guts all over my shoe." Annalisa pulled open the huge refrigerator, which was so tall and wide it looked more like it belonged in a restaurant than in someone's kitchen, even if those someones were the Arnolds. She retrieved another of the blue bottles like the one she'd handed to Rascal. The label was unfamiliar to her. She'd seen plenty of beer commercials, but this stuff was some kind of import. *Kronenbourg*, she read. *Brewed in Obernai, France.*

France!

"What kind of beer is this, anyway? I've never even heard of it."

"It's from France. The liquor store imports them for Daddy. When he was there with Mom a few years ago, he discovered it and really liked it." Brooklyn wrinkled her nose. "I think it smells like a skunk's butt."

Annalisa giggled. "Good thing you don't have to drink it."

"Ugh. No thank you."

"Did you guys get to go to France too?"

"No. It was during school, so we had to stay. Mom was trying to hire a live-in nanny, but she couldn't find anyone who wanted to babysit three parahuman kids. Then she found Carson, and he was great. He let us have ice cream every day while Mom and Daddy were gone."

Annalisa nodded. "Sounds like the kind of thing he would do. What was it like when they came back?"

Brooklyn sniffed. "It was stupid. Mom didn't have a good showing so she was mad. Daddy was mad a lot too. He was always yelling at us and at Mom. At first we thought they were going to get divorced."

"So what happened?"

Brooklyn shrugged. "They worked it out, I guess. They stopped arguing. Daddy got a promotion to investigative reporter and after that things went a lot better. He was probably just stressed out about work, you know?"

"Yeah, I guess." Annalisa twisted off the bottle cap with her bare hands. "We better go give this to your dad before he starts investigating why we didn't."

"Heh. You're funny, Annalisa. Brianna and Brittany aren't funny like you are. They don't make me smile. They're just annoying. Brianna thinks she's hilarious." Brooklyn lowered her voice to a whisper. "She's not."

"Hey, Brookie, can I ask you something?" Annalisa lowered her own voice. Maybe this would be her chance to build some rapport with one of the Culture Club.

"You know, I hate that nickname." Brooklyn grimaced in discontent.

"Why? I'm sorry, I won't call you . . . it . . . again."

"When we were a lot younger, Daddy had all his pet names for us. We used to be Britt, Bree, and Brook. Then he stopped calling us those for awhile. Maybe he thought they sounded too grown-up or something. Now he calls us Brittie, Brainy, and Brookie. I mean, we sound like we're kittens or something."

"The other two don't mind it?"

"No, but I'm different." Brooklyn twisted her inhumanly flexible face into a rictus of a smile. "I have a dark soul."

Annalisa's phone buzzed. She glanced down at it. It was a message from Wheels. *The package has been delivered.* She blinked, surprised that their plan had worked even though it hadn't been particularly clever. "Hey, this is my mom. I have to go. It's still a school night."

Brooklyn shrugged. "Okay. We're so close to the end of the year, does it really matter?"

"It matters to her. And it matters to me too. I'm going to go to the Hero Academy someday. I can't start slacking off now."

"That sounds pretty cool. I don't think we'll ever do that."

"Why not?"

"There's no way mom and dad would ever let us. They can't lose control over us. We're their child stars."

Annalisa hesitated, then squeezed Brooklyn's hand for a second. "I'm sorry," she whispered. "I really do have to go."

Brooklyn nodded. "I get it. See you tomorrow, Anna."

"You know how you hate *Brookie*? I hate *Anna*."

"So what do you prefer?"

"*Capitána*. Or Annalisa."

"Fine." Brooklyn slipped past her with her dad's beer. "Hey you guys, Annalisa has to go."

Brianna and Brittany's chorus of "Awww!" was perfectly pitched for maximum false disappointment.

"You need a ride home, Anna?" asked Ben Arnold.

"No thank you. I'll fly. It's faster and there aren't any sketchy vans that say *Free Candy* fifty feet up."

Arnold laughed with a booming chuckle that almost sounded forced to Annalisa's ears. "Anyway, thanks for the pizza. I'll see you guys in school tomorrow. *Auw revoyer!*" She'd looked up the French words for *goodbye* before coming to visit the Culture Club and listened carefully to Google's pronunciation. Then she intentionally mangled it, just to see.

"*Au revoir*," said Arnold as quickly as if Annalisa had written it into a script. He pronounced it like Google had: *ohr vwar*.

Like a native would have.

Chapter Twenty-Two

Annalisa raced across the city as fast as she could fly, her fists clenched over her head in an attempt to keep herself as aerodynamic as possible. She didn't really understand the concept of it, but everything she'd ever seen on TV confirmed *that* was the way to fly faster. She didn't know if she was actually going any faster, but it *felt* faster. The air whipped her hair behind her as she zeroed in on the cluttered rust-brown patch that was Wheels' place. Even though she had her regular clothes on instead of her superhero costume, she felt more heroic than she ever had as she plummeted down from the unimaginable height of a hundred feet to slam to the dirt beside the Neighborhood Watch headquarters. A great cloud of dust billowed skyward in the wake of her impact, and a perfectly round crater a couple inches deep spread out around her landing crouch.

Breezy and Hothead burst out of the trailer, one swirling dust devils around his hands and the other's head burning like a torch, ready to defend their world against villains real or imagined. When they saw Annalisa amid the expansive dust, they relaxed.

"Dude, you shook the entire Winnebago," said Breezy. "We thought it was supervillains or somethin'."

"Maybe someday," said Annalisa. "Then we'll fight them off. Is Carson here?"

"Yeah." Hothead concentrated, clenching his fists until his head-flames died out. "He's doing the genetic test thingie right now."

"Cool." Annalisa brushed dust off her legs and feet. "Listen, I think Carson is onto something with that French guy. Ben Arnold speaks French like he's from a movie. I said something wrong on purpose and he corrected me without even thinking."

"You really think he went and killed their real dad?" asked Breezy. "That's messed up."

"Yeah, it is, and yeah, I do." Annalist frowned. She went into the headquarters with the boys right behind her. Carson was sitting at Wheels' workbench, working with what looked like a combination of a tiny chemistry set and a tablet computer. Wheels herself sat as close as she possibly could to the PRA agent, firing off a nonstop litany of questions about what he was doing and how everything worked. He answered her with the patience of a saint, something he'd likely gained working for the Arnold family.

Rascal was lying against the ceiling where he wouldn't be in the way, using his powers to stick to it. He had an open bottle of Coke with a straw in it and was sipping from it when Annalisa walked in. He grinned at her. "Heard you show up. Almost shook me loose. That was real slick how you got that bottle."

"You're just lucky nobody saw you," said Annalisa. "That would have caused all kinds of problems."

"Nah. I'm a known troublemaker." He swirled his Coke. "They'd just figure I was there for that."

"You don't know that. The triplets aren't as dumb as you all think they are."

Carson looked over his shoulder at them. "Nobody is saying they're not bright. They're very intelligent, but they do live in a bit of a sheltered environment, and their mother rules with an iron fist."

"How long until your DNA test is done?" Annalisa crowded in behind Wheels, hovering above to see better.

"A few more minutes. It would go a little faster if someone hadn't contaminated the sample with his own DNA." Carson shot a good-natured glare upward toward Rascal.

"Hey, you didn't want me to drop it, and that meant I had to stick it to me. You got my DNA so it's easy enough."

"I have to strip out all the DNA records of everyone who's touched this bottle," said Carson. "That means you, whoever picked it up at the store and whoever else may have handled it during distribution and manufacturing. Luckily, we're searching for a specific positive match, so if it doesn't turn up, we can assume that Ben Arnold is not who he claims to be."

"I don't understand," said Hothead. "All that from him just drinking out of it?" He looked at his own bottle of soda as if it might jump up and bite him.

"It's like this, Cole . . ." Wheels spun her chair around to face him. "Say instead of DNA, you've got a bottle that's splattered with a bunch of different colors of paint, and you're checking to see if one of them is a specific blue, and you've got a color swatch to match up. Either that blue is on there or it isn't. If it is, you know Ben Arnold is really Ben Arnold. If it isn't, you know it's that French guy."

"Well, we don't actually *know* it would be the French guy," said Carson. "He just happens to be the most likely possibility." He looked at his tablet. "It's not looking good for Arnold, though. I'm down to the last five or six discrete DNA samples on this bottle and they're all old and incomplete, but none of them are matching up to what I have on file for Arnold."

"So what happens now?" asked Annalisa. "We know he's not who he says he is. Can we go arrest him?"

"No, not yet. We don't have any evidence that he's committed a crime. All we can prove is that he's lying about his identity, but that in and of itself is not illegal."

"But he murdered the real Mr. Arnold, didn't he?" asked Breezy.

"We can't prove that." Carson's tablet made a pinging noise and he looked down and nodded. "However, I can prove that he's definitely not Ben Arnold. Bag up that bottle for me, would you, Wheels? That is now evidence."

Wheels, her hands wrapped in rubber gloves, sealed up the bottle into a quart bag. "We have to catch him doing something illegal. He was going to rob a bank, right? Don't you think he'll try it again?"

Annalisa shook her head. "He was doing it so the triplets could catch him. They were *supposed* to bust him. That would have gotten them a lot of publicity. That's what they're after."

"Or what their mother is after," said Carson. "As I said, she pretty much runs that household. The triplets might be as much victims of this as everyone else. They're like child stars of TV and movies. There are numerous horror stories out there about how kid stars have their lives ruined by their parents trying to capitalize off their success." He sighed. "And the truth is, I'm pretty fond of them after the past few years of cooking and cleaning. They're not horrible people. They're spoiled, but that doesn't make them awful." He paused. "Well, not all the time, anyway."

"We gotta tell them," said Breezy. Everyone looked at him. "What? If their dad's dead, they gotta know about it. It ain't fair if we keep it from them. I'd want to know if mine was dead, even if I ain't seen him in ten years."

"Yeah, you're right," said Annalisa. "I should tell them."

"No, *we* should tell them," said Carson. "They'll believe me. And I want to be involved. This is bigger than just the three of them." He pulled his phone out of his pocket and touched a button on it. "Hey, it's me. We need to have Paris authorities exhume that body and get a DNA sample from it. I'm pretty sure we'll discover it's Ben Arnold . . . Yeah, I know . . . Right, I love you too." He hung up and looked at Annalisa and the others. "All right, we've set a chain of events in motion. All that remains is to see it through to the end."

"I've got an idea," said Wheels. "Capitána is already in good with the triplets. After you guys tell them the truth, you should work with them to try to set up another fake robbery. Only this time, we'll all be ready for it, and we'll have the cops ready too. We'll catch him in the act, and they'll arrest him. They'll know about his powers this time, so they can be ready for that too."

"As a parahuman, he'd be subject to holding at Deep Six while awaiting his trial." Carson scratched his jaw. Annalisa knew Deep Six was the parahuman prison in Montana. She hoped she would get to visit it someday. "And that's if he didn't get extradited to France."

"What's *exturdited*?" asked Hothead.

"It means he gets sent back to France to face the charges of crimes he committed there," said Carson. "We'll have to be careful about not giving him the route of an entrapment defense."

"What does that even mean?" Hothead's hair was beginning to smolder, suggesting he'd run out of patience with the legalese.

"It's complicated. Don't worry, if we can prove he planned and committed the first robbery, he doesn't have a leg to stand on in court if we catch him after the second." Carson pulled out his phone. "I'm going to have to consult with our legal team on this one to make sure we do everything right." He looked down at Annalisa. "I'll meet the triplets with you. Name the time and the place and I'll be there."

Annalisa already had a spot in mind. "Okay," she said. "But I don't think you're going to like it."

Chapter Twenty-Three

The Events Center was further away from her home than Annalisa had ever flown before, especially when carrying a shivering Carson like an oversized baby doll. She'd Googled overhead images of it so she'd know it when she saw it, and the GPS on her phone still worked when she was flying, so she wasn't worried about her ability to find the building.

She chose such a distant location from home because the chances of accidentally running across Ben Arnold were vanishingly small. If she'd picked someplace immediately local to the triplets, they might not have taken her request to meet seriously at all. When she'd selected a public landmark like the Events Center that was several miles away from the center of town, she knew it would pique their curiosity. Also, she'd checked the schedule and knew they weren't likely to run across anyone as it was two days after one concert and three days before the next one.

The sun was already low over the mountains behind her as she flew over fields and tech industry facilities with their expanses of shining white cement and manicured grounds. She'd eschewed the costume the triplets designed for her and felt better about her green t-shirt and red cape flapping against her shoulders as she sped through the sky.

"F-f-for the last time, you c-could land and I'd d-drive us." Carson had alternated between squeezing his eyes shut so as not to see anything and keeping them open as wide as possible when he couldn't stand not seeing any longer.

"We'll be late if we do that. Besides, somebody could follow your car."

"You mean Mr. Arnold?"

"He can change his face. You'd never know it was him."

"We could have r-rented one. Why do you have to fly so high?"

"I want anyone who sees me to think I'm a bird."

Carson chuckled in spite of his fear. "Annalisa, nobody could ever mistake you for a bird."

She glared at him. "I could drop you, Carson."

"Oh God, please don't!"

It was her turn to chuckle. "I wouldn't. Not ever. Now turn that phone so I can see it better."

Carson tilted her phone that he held in a death grip back so she could see the screen.

"We're close. Hey, there it is. It looks like a big upside-down bread pan." She pointed and Carson shifted just enough in her arms to squeak like someone far smaller. "Oh, lighten up. You're as bad as . . . well, as someone who's terrible at flying."

"I *am* terrible at flying. Nobody said this would be a part of the job when the PRA recruited me."

"Highway," said Annalisa, and they flew over I-25. A couple of horns honked in her wake and she knew someone had seen them, but that wasn't a big deal. There was no way Ben Arnold would know about this meeting unless the triplets had told him, and Annalisa had learned the girls didn't like to share anything with their parents unless absolutely necessary. The Events Center was just beyond the highway. She angled down over the parking lot and landed on the flat spot at the apex of the large cushion-shaped dome over the arena. There was a framework along the center line that contained some kind of ventilation or lighting or something— Annalisa didn't know what—but that was where she had told the triplets she would meet them. A safety rail encircled the entire framework, so she felt comfortable that Carson wouldn't accidentally plunge over the side. "Hey, open your eyes, we're here." She set Carson down on the flat surface as gently as she could and he staggered over to the rail to hang over it. "Hey, are you going to be sick?"

He shook his head. "No. I just need a minute. Holy crap, that was terrifying."

"Carson?" Annalisa looked up toward the source of the voice and saw the three Arnold sisters staring down at them, mouths agape. Brittany had her arms around her two sisters and Brooklyn had stretched hers around all three to make an organic safety harness. The three of them likewise dropped to the rooftop, shocked into silence.

"Hi, girls."

Brittany stepped forward suddenly, her fists cocked. "Did you kidnap him, Anna? Because he's ours, and we'll fight you right now."

Annalisa didn't move. "He's not yours. He's not mine. He's his own. Tell them who you are, Carson. Who you are *really*."

Carson nodded and pulled his badge out of his pocket. "Girls, I'm from the Parahuman Resources Agency. I've been on a long-term assignment to monitor you and the other parahuman children here in Loveland."

"You're what? You're not really a cook?" Brianna stepped up beside her sister, encouraging Brittany to lower her fists.

"Well, I am. I mean, I've really been doing all the things for you that your parents hired me to do, but I'm also with the Parahuman Resources Agency."

"Why are you here now? And why are we having this meeting all the way up here? Although it is kind of cool." Brooklyn stretched her neck much further than possible so she could get a better view of the surrounding countryside.

"We've got some bad news about your dad." Annalisa glanced at Carson. They'd decided she should be the one to deliver the initial news, and Carson would back her up.

Brittany crossed her arms. "What kind of news?"

Annalisa took a deep breath. "The man you think is your father isn't. Your real father is dead. He was murdered when he went to Paris with your mom."

Brittany and Brianna looked at each other and laughed. "That's crazy," said Brianna. "What are you smoking, Anna?"

"Your real father called you Bree and Britt and Brook. Please, you have to believe me."

"Come on, girls," said Brittany, reaching for her sisters. "Let's go home and watch *Rooftops*."

"No." Brooklyn didn't move.

"Come on, Brookie," said Brianna.

"No. I want to hear what they have to say." She crossed her arms and looked at her sisters. "Prove what you're saying is true and I'll believe you."

Carson held out his tablet. "These are two genetic charts. The one on the left is your father's. I took a sample from him just before he and your mother left for Paris for the fashion show in 2015. The one on the right is the one Annalisa brought us yesterday."

Brittany's eyes widened. "The beer bottle? That's why you offered to bring him one?"

Annalisa nodded.

Carson swiped one of the charts away. "There was an unsolved murder during Fashion Week in

Paris. An unidentified male was found nearby. He'd been, uh, damaged so it was impossible to identify him by conventional means. Luckily, French authorities were able to obtain DNA information before the body was committed to a pauper's grave. They never had any leads so that information didn't ever get matched up. I had them send it to me this morning." He brought up a second DNA chart next to the one from the triplets' father. "Girls, I'm very sorry to tell you that your father didn't come home from Paris. Someone else did, pretending to be him."

A tear rolled down Brooklyn's cheek. "I always wondered. He seemed so different when he came home. Remember? That's when we thought they were going to get divorced. They fought all the time, about everything."

Brianna reached out to hug Brooklyn. "It's so much to take in. I mean, it's hard to believe when he's there all the time, but yeah, maybe I do see it now."

Brittany turned away from the others, her fists clenched. "No. That's not fair. He's our *dad*. He loves us. He tells us all the time. He wants us to be great."

"No, Bree, he wants us to be *famous*. They both do. Him and mom." Brooklyn wiped her eyes. "Do you think she knows?"

"Oh God, what if she does? What if she's known all along?" asked Brianna.

Annalisa looked at Carson. She had no idea what to do or say. From the look of utter helplessness on his face, lips curled down and brow furrowed, neither did he.

Brittany grabbed the railing and tore a piece loose. With an anguished shriek, she hurled it over the side.

"Crap!" cried Carson. "Don't do that!"

Brittany whirled around and punched a piece of the steel framework, denting it hard enough to bend it inward. Something made of glass fell nearby and shattered.

"Brittany, stop it!" said Annalisa. "You're going to hurt someone!"

Brittany looked back over her shoulder. "Yes, you're right. Someone I should have hurt a long time ago." She flung herself into the sky, flying back toward town like some furious bird of prey.

"She's going after Arnold. Or Chrétien. Whoever he is really." Carson looked down at Annalisa. "You have to stop her, Annalisa, before she does something she'll regret for the rest of her life."

Annalisa realized it was time for her to step up and do what she'd dreamed of for years: be a superhero.

She launched herself after Brittany.

Chapter Twenty-four

"Brittany, stop! Please!" Annalisa called into the growing darkness. She could barely see Brittany's dark costume against the deep indigo of the mountains. She dipped lower until she was flying low enough to see Brittany against the orange and pink clouds of sunset. Doing so placed her in peril of flying into a building or tree or even a light pole. She tried to keep one eye on her path while still following the fleeing Arnold sister.

"Come on, Capitána, get it together," Annalisa muttered. "You've got to be the faster one tonight." And somehow, she managed to eke a bit more speed out of her powers. As the blocks raced past beneath them, she gained on Brittany, inch by inch. It was exhausting, straining herself beyond her limits the way she was. Who would have thought flying took so much effort?

As they raced over the lake, Annalisa caught up to Brittany and grabbed hold of the other girl's heel. "Got you!"

Brittany kicked at her but Annalisa hung on with dogged determination. She locked one hand around Brittany's ankle and pulled her back and down while using her other hand to fend off the kicks aimed at her face. "Let me go!" screamed Brittany.

Annalisa started to say *no* but one of Brittany's kicks connected square across her mouth. She gasped and lost hold of the other girl's heel. Red spots flashed in her vision and she felt like she'd bitten her tongue. It wasn't painful the way it would have been for someone else getting kicked in the face. A normal person could hit Annalisa and she would feel the blow, but it wouldn't hurt her. Brittany's kick didn't hurt her either, but it made her teeth rattle in her head and got her anger pumping.

Still, she couldn't let Brittany fly home, perhaps to murder the man that until a few minutes ago she'd thought was her father. Annalisa didn't know a lot of things about people, but she figured killing a parent would scar someone for life. And as a hero, she would do whatever she could to prevent that, even if it meant taking one for the proverbial team.

She lunged after Brittany, her nose running from the kick to the face, and caught her once again. Instead of grabbing Brittany's heel, she wrapped her hand around the other girl's ankle and pulled. "Not . . . letting you . . . go!"

Annalisa had never fought anyone while flying. Well, to be fair, she'd never fought anyone period. Her parents had reinforced with her time and time again her strength was every bit as dangerous and lethal to an unpowered opponent as a gun. Brittany, on the other hand, was super-strong and tough like Annalisa, and it seemed like as good a time as any to learn a bit about scrapping. She pulled Brittany toward her with a fist cocked back to deliver a punch.

She realized far too late that she'd left herself wide open as Brittany shoved her back and down toward the lake. "Leave me alone!" cried the Arnold sister. Annalisa felt lake water soak her feet and struggled to fly back toward Brittany, who'd stopped her headlong flight to stare at Annalisa after her shove.

Annalisa struck Brittany like a cannonball, driving her shoulder into the triplet's midriff, sending them both spinning through the air. It was a textbook flying tackle, except they kept right on flying out over the lake. Brittany struck at Annalisa's back and shoulders. Annalisa felt every blow but like the earlier kick, none of them hurt. Then Brittany grabbed a handful of Annalisa's hair and pulled her head back. A hard punch caught Annalisa across the jaw and a twinge of pain raced across her face and down her spine. She shook her head to clear it and this time tasted blood in her mouth. Was her super-toughness failing her?

Before she had time to think what to do next, Brittany drove her knee into Annalisa's pelvis and they spun apart.

Pain radiated from Annalisa's side. She didn't feel like she'd gotten any weaker, but her ability to soak up impacts was definitely reducing as her fight with Brittany went on. She had to end it soon or she might suffer a real injury. She launched herself back at Brittany, trying to wrestle the other girl's arms against her sides. "You have to stop," she hissed through clenched teeth.

"I'm going to kill him, and you can't do a thing to stop me." Brittany shrugged herself free of Annalisa's grasp and tore away Annalisa's cape. The clasp parted at Annalisa's throat and Brittany flung away the piece of red cloth. "And I hate that stupid cape."

Annalisa, more mad than she'd ever been in her life, grabbed hold of Brittany, spun around in midair once, and hurled her toward the ground with all her might. "That was *my* cape!" she cried.

Brittany spun out of control and crashed through the roof of the boat house at the side of the lake. At first, Annalisa was proud of the massive blow she'd delivered. She flew down to the hole, but when Brittany didn't burst right back out to continue the battle, she peered over the edge into the darkness below. "Brittany?"

After what seemed like years of waiting, Annalisa heard a shuddering sniffle in response.

"Are you okay?" She patted around herself and found her phone, luckily still in her back pocket and undamaged despite the pounding she had both delivered and received. She checked her charge. It was only at forty-eight percent, but that should be enough. She turned on the flashlight app and shone it down into the boathouse.

Brittany knelt on a splintered dock, debris from her impact scattered around her. She had her face in her hands and was sobbing.

Annalisa floated down into the drifting dust to settle down beside Brittany. "Brittany?"

Brittany glanced over at her. Her eyes were rimmed with red and she had a bruise forming over one eye where Annalisa must have gotten in a solid blow. She felt guilty for a moment but that feeling vanished over her more genuine concern for Brittany. The triplet might not have been a good friend, but at least she was a fellow parahuman and classmate and she was suffering in a way Annalisa could only imagine. "I'm s-sorry about your cape. I know it was important to you."

"It's okay. I can always make another one. Or maybe I won't. Capes are kind of old-fashioned."

Brittany wiped her eyes. "No, you should wear one. You should always wear it. You're a better superhero than any of us."

Annalisa shrugged. "I'm just trying to do the right thing."

"Daddy—I mean, whoever he is—said it was for the publicity. Nobody was going to get hurt. He was going to arrange for someone to pretend to rob a bank and we would stop him and then he would cover it on the news. We were going to be famous. Not just here, but nationwide. It was going to get us on TV, or into the movies. Mom already has an agent for us."

"Did she know? Was she in on the plan?"

"I don't know. He never talked about it with anyone but us."

Annalisa frowned. She wasn't sure how to proceed. "We should go back and talk to Carson."

"I really want to kill him, Anna."

"Carson?"

"No. That . . . man."

An idea came to Annalisa as suddenly as if someone had turned on an overhead spotlight. "No, we can do better. We can catch him and *extradite* him."

"What does that mean?"

"We send him back to France to stand trial for murdering your real father."

"How do we do that?"

Annalisa lifted herself off the ground to hover over Brittany. "I got an idea. Come on."

Brittany flew after her through the hole in the boathouse roof. They hovered over the roof for a moment, looking down at the damage they'd wrought upon the innocent wooden building. "Wow, we really messed it up. You think we'll get in trouble?"

"Maybe we can volunteer to help fix it."

"We don't have to tell them it was us." Brittany looked at her.

"Yes, we do." Annalisa was emphatic.

"Well, okay." They turned and headed back toward the events center where the others were. "So I really can't kill him?" Brittany called.

"Nope."

"Can I at least hurt him a little?"

"We'll talk."

Chapter Twenty-Five

With just over a week left in the school year, most students were either focusing on their final exams and projects or completely blowing them off in favor of their upcoming extended period of goofing off. Unfortunately, Annalisa and the rest of the Neighborhood Watch couldn't enjoy the last days of the year with their upcoming operation to catch the man they had taken to calling *L'imposteur.* Neither were they focusing on their tests or projects, and when Wheels announced sadly at lunch that she'd failed her science final, Annalisa knew they were all going to have to sacrifice more than they'd ever considered.

The Culture Club had kept discreetly quiet, staying away from the Neighborhood Watch and avoiding their typical bullying patterns of behavior. They didn't want to attract any more attention as they waited for all the pieces of the plan to fall into place.

The plan was a real doozy, as Breezy had called it. They were going to have to convince *L'imposteur* to perform another staged bank robbery, this time with the Culture Club stopping it as planned. Once they did so, the police would sweep in on them, led by officers Velez and Bickle. Carson and Torvald would ensure *L'imposteur* would be hauled away to Deep Six pending his extradition to France. At least, that was the idea, but it was taking French authorities forever to match the DNA they'd collected from the murder victim with the information Carson had sent to them. Once they did, though, the case against *L'imposteur* would be as airtight as they could make it.

In the meantime, they waited.

Annalisa floated through her afternoon classes in a fog, like she'd come down with the flu. She couldn't concentrate on her work, made stupid mistakes on her tests, forgot everything she'd ever read in her textbooks, until it seemed every one of her teachers was exasperated with her. Whenever she saw the triplets in the hall, she nodded their way. Brittany had withdrawn into herself following their tussle, and it seemed Brianna had taken over de facto leadership of the Culture Club. She kept things low-key, ignoring freshmen and upper classmen alike. Only Brooklyn seemed unfazed by the news that the man they thought was their father was an impostor and maybe even a murderer. Maybe it was because she wasn't as close to him as her sisters, or maybe it was, as she said, the darkness in her soul. Whatever the reason, Annalisa hoped her steadfastness was helping her sisters cope as they waited to hear from Carson.

After school, Annalisa skipped her bus. Instead, she went for walk, wandering around the school grounds until she found herself sitting on the bleachers of the empty football field, wishing she had someone to talk to but wanting to be alone at the same time.

She wasn't there for more than a minute or two before she saw Breezy, loping up the steps toward her. "Hey, Breezy."

"Hey, Capitána. What're you doin'?"

"Just hanging out. Thinking."

He sat beside her. "Thinkin' 'bout what?"

"Are we doing the right thing? This whole crazy plan to catch a real supervillain. It's all . . . Scooby-Doo."

"Scooby-Doo?"

"Yeah, you know. *I'd have gotten away with it if it wasn't for you kids.* That's us this time, right?"

"Maybe. I can eat a pizza like Shaggy."

Annalisa laughed.

"Naw, we're doin' the right thing. If this dude killed the triplets' dad, he needs to pay for his crime. If he didn't, he's still been lyin' to them for years. That ain't right either. We got to put a stop to it, or we ain't no kind of heroes."

Annalisa laid her head against his shoulder. "This feels like it ought to be someone else doing it. We're just a bunch of kids. We should be playing video games and riding bikes and stuff, not saving the world."

"We ain't savin' the world. We're just helpin' make our town a better place." Breezy looked around. "I mean, it ain't that bad now, but we can make it better, right?"

"Don't ever change, Breezy. You've got a great way of looking at the world."

From somewhere deep in his belly, Breezy summoned a resounding belch. Both kids dissolved into giggles.

Both their phones buzzed with an incoming message. Very few people would send simultaneous messages to both of them, which mean it was Neighborhood Watch business. Annalisa unlocked her screen to read the message. It was from Carson. *Paris medical examiner confirmed unidentified victim in France was Ben Arnold.*

Annalisa looked up from her screen at Breezy. "Looks like it's on."

He nodded. "On like Donkey Kong."

She stood. "Do you have your cape?"

He shook his head. "It's at home, in my room. Do you have yours?"

"It's at the bottom of the lake where Brittany threw it. But I don't need mine to fly. I'll carry you, Breezy."

Breezy looked around, maybe checking to see if anyone was watching them. "Naw, it's cool. I'll just run home."

"Don't be stupid, Breezy. It's got to be like ninety-five degrees out here. You'll kill yourself. Or else you'll be all gross and sweaty and nobody will want you in the headquarters until you take a shower."

Their phones buzzed again, this time with an alert from the Neighborhood Watch app. Wheels was calling in the troops.

"Breezy, get over yourself. You don't have to be all *macho* all the time. It's okay to let a girl carry you."

"Yeah, but . . . aw, shoot. I guess I don't have a good reason. Just as far as my house so I can get my cape, okay?"

"Deal." Annalisa held out her arms. "*La Capitána* Flight 100 to Breezy's house, now boarding."

"Ma-a-a-an . . ." Breezy looked around once more, then climbed into Annalisa's waiting arms like he was a blushing bride about to be carried through the doorway of a newlyweds' house. He locked his arms around Annalisa's neck. "Don't drop me."

"You guys are always saying that," said Annalisa. "You're going to give me ideas." Nevertheless, she made sure to hold onto him extra tight as she launched from the bleachers. The world spiraled beneath her as she wheeled about to orient herself, then transitioned to horizontal flight, making a beeline for Breezy's house.

It was kind of nice flying with Breezy, she thought. He wasn't afraid of heights, being a flyer himself, and he understood the intricacies of parahuman flight. He leaned when needed without being told. He relaxed in Annalisa's arms without becoming a floppy burden, allowing her to adjust his position when she needed to without struggling. She could have carried him all day if it came down to it.

Breezy's house wasn't far, and she landed gently in the front yard. It was a well-kept yard and house, even though it was tiny and in a poor neighborhood. Breezy's mom was proud of her place, and it showed from the well-swept sidewalk to the flowers in the front window box. "I'll be right back. Just gotta grab my cape." He winced as he said *cape*. "Aw, shoot. I'm sorry, Annalisa. You probably all sensitive about it, huh?"

Annalisa shook her head. "Maybe I will be later, Breezy. It's just a cape. I can always make another one. If I even bother. There are a lot of downsides to capes."

"Maybe so, but you ain't gonna feel right without one."

Annalisa smiled. "You're probably right, Breezy. Hurry up and change."

Breezy smiled back at her and dashed inside. Annalisa floated back and forth across the lawn without touching it—the equivalent of pacing for her. After a couple of minutes, the front door bashed open and she turned to see Breezy, his cape gathered up over his shoulders, laden with a bag of garbage. "Sorry, just a minute. Got a chore to do or I'll be on punishment." He pulled the lid off the big green garbage can on the side of the house and threw the bag inside. He went back to the front door and poked his head inside. "Okay, Ma. Can I go?"

Annalisa clearly heard "Not until you wash your hands, young man," from inside. She giggled as Breezy made an exasperated noise and ran back inside. He emerged a moment later, wiping his hands on his shirt.

"Why aren't you wearing your costume?" asked Annalisa, taking in his basketball tank top and baggy shorts.

"It's laundry day. For reals this time."

They laughed as they sprang into the sky.

Chapter Twenty-Six

The rest of the Neighborhood Watch was already at the headquarters and instead of being cramped inside with Carson and Torvald, they were sitting in the shade on one side of the Winnebago, drinking Cokes and fanning themselves when Annalisa and Breezy arrived. A Styrofoam cooler filled with ice and red-labeled bottles sat next to the Winnebago steps.

"Headquarters AC is borked," said Wheels almost before Breezy's cape had settled. "You think it's hot out here, you should see what it's like in there. Now I know what a microwave burrito feels like." A makeshift fan was plugged into her wheelchair's battery, clamped to an armature, and blew into her face.

"We tried to fix it," said Hothead. He hadn't bothered to wear his costume and looked like a pale redheaded chihuahua as he sprawled in the dust beside the headquarters. "But some of us are into practical jokes and some of us are definitely not." He glared over at Rascal, who'd stripped off everything but his pants. Sweat glistened on the boy's tautly muscular torso, and Annalisa was surprised to see he even had a six-pack. Skateboarding must have been a better full-body workout than she'd thought.

"Someday, you'll discover that long-lost sense of humor, Cole, and then you'll laugh and laugh." Rascal held his Coke bottle against an angry red spot on one shoulder that looked like it might have been a burn.

"Geez, you guys. Maybe we should go somewhere cooler," said Annalisa.

"I could let you back into the school, but if anybody saw, there would be some uncomfortable questions," said Torvald. "It's the kind of thing that could get me suspended."

"Yeah, but you don't work for the school. You work for the PRA," said Hothead.

"I still work for the school. I'm not a fake librarian. I have a real degree in library sciences, in fact. And I don't particularly want to lose that job. You know, I kind of like it."

"Yo, are there any more Cokes?" asked Breezy. Rascal tossed him one. "Thanks, bro."

Annalisa was thirsty too, but she felt more like a water. She ducked into the headquarters to take a bottle from the mini fridge. It was like stepping into an oven, and she hurried back outside.

"So what's the plan?" asked Rascal.

"We wait." Wheels brushed an errant lock of hair away from her face.

"For what?"

"For them." Annalisa pointed into the sky. The triplets were approaching, much the same way she'd seen them travel before with Brittany lifting the other two.

They landed in the dust in front of the Winnebago and looked around in obvious dismay and not a little disgust. "*This* is where you meet?" asked Brittany. "It's a frickin' junkyard." Annalisa felt her cheeks grow hot. Compared to what the triplets had back at their home, the proud headquarters of the Neighborhood Watch must have looked like a dirty pile of trash. And if she looked at it objectively, she had to admit it kind of did.

"Hey, beautiful," said Rascal. "Do I come to your house and tell you about the appalling state of your upstairs bathroom?" He grinned at the newcomers. "It looks like a gooey glitter bomb went off in there."

Brianna's mouth fell open. "How do you know that? I mean, uh, no it doesn't."

Rascal climbed up the side of the Winnebago and rolled along it until his back was stuck to the side while his arms and legs splayed out. "You can't expect me to do the spider thing on your walls and not look around. By the way, my initials are somewhere on the outside of your house.

Lemme know when you find them." He held up his sharpie and smiled.

Brittany stepped forward, fire in her eyes, her hands clenching into fists. "I ought to—"

Carson stepped between them. "Nobody ought to anything. Let's all remember that right now, we're all on the same side. We're all trying to catch the same criminal, and he's a killer, in case you forgot." He crossed his arms. "You need to take this seriously." He glanced back over his shoulder at Rascal. "All of you."

Rascal shrugged. "Call them like I see them, boss."

"Don't call me that."

Torvald leaned down to whisper to Annalisa. "I love it when he takes charge."

"You guys want a soda?" Breezy rummaged through the ice in the cooler. "There's Coke, and . . . more Coke."

"Guess I'll have a Coke, then," said Brianna.

"Me too," said Brittany.

"I'll just suffer, thanks," said Brooklyn.

Brittany stamped her foot. "Just take the damn Coke, Brook. That way I don't have to listen to you complain how thirsty you are all the way back to the house."

The tension between the three sisters was so thick, Annalisa felt like she could have punched it and it would have resisted. Clearly, having a supervillain impersonate their father was causing a lot of stress. She couldn't really blame them. She didn't even want to think how she would react to the same circumstances.

"All right, everyone, let's start at the beginning so we're all on the same page for the end," said Carson. "Three years ago, Ben Arnold traveled to Paris with his wife, your mother, as her guest for the Paris Fashion Show. He never returned. A body was found in Paris during the show, and someone had taken great care to remove or alter identifying characteristics to make it exceptionally difficult to identify the victim with conventional means. The best Paris police could manage was to take DNA samples and hope they would find a match."

"The problem with that technique is there has to be a baseline sample in a system somewhere they can match. The real Ben Arnold lived a fairly uneventful life as a reporter before meeting his wife, your mother. He never traveled abroad, never got into any kind of trouble. There was no reason his DNA would be on file anywhere. When we first got into town and our local positions, Carson managed to get a DNA sample off him, much the same way you did, Annalisa. We ran a test screening on it primarily to check for the Musashi gene and when it came back negative, we were at a loss to explain why the three of you—"

"Eight of us," interrupted Annalisa. "You said none of our parents have the Musashi gene either."

"Yes, eight of you. We couldn't explain why you have the powers you do, and honestly still can't. That's why the PRA assigned us to long-term duty here in Loveland."

"Someone flew back to the States with Barbara Arnold," continued Carson. "He looked like Ben Arnold, sounded like Ben Arnold, and maybe even acted like him a little. But we believe most likely he is this man." He held up his tablet so everyone could see the image of the sharp-nosed man with the wide-set eyes and weak jawline. "Gérard Chrétien, known to French authorities as *Le Masque*. He has the ability to change his appearance and as an actor, is skilled at pretending to be someone he is not."

"The problem is we have no definitive way to identify him with his parahuman abilities. He can appear as *anyone*, and there's no way to know for sure what his true face is," said Torvald. "The only way to be sure it's him is through genetic testing. Thanks to Annalisa and the rest of you, we have an accurate genetic sample to match him to, but it's unlikely the French authorities will be able to tie him to the murder of your father, girls."

"Wait, you mean he's going to get away with it?" Brittany clenched her fists. If she'd had the ability to catch herself on fire the way Hothead did, Annalisa was pretty sure she'd be nothing but a ball of flame.

"In the short term, yes, I'm afraid so," said Carson. "But there's hope, and this is why we're going to plan very carefully. If we can catch him in the commission of a crime and detain him, we have enough circumstantial evidence to hold him at Deep Six due to his powers. They have a psi on staff who can read his mind. Mind scans are not admissible evidence in U. S. courts, but French law permits them if they are obtained in reference to guide investigators in their process."

"What does that even mean?" asked Hothead.

"It means the psi can search for information in Chrétien's mind related to the murder of Ben Arnold, and if there's anything, they can give French investigators some suggestions on leads to pursue or evidence to seek. So long as the investigators are the ones to find the key to implicate him, the case can proceed." Torvald shrugged. "It's pretty deep and complex for me, never mind the rest of you.

"The bottom line is that to tie him to your father's murder, we need to catch him in the act of a crime, and that's where you guys come in." Carson looked at the triplets. "Girls, you need to convince him to try his plan again, or at least a version of it. Get him to rob a bank, or something like it, but it won't be the three of you busting him, it will be the police."

"And us," said Wheels. "We're not sitting this one out. You wouldn't have anything at all if not for Annalisa. And she's our teammate." She looked at Brittany. "The Neighborhood Watch has your back on this one, Culture Club."

Brittany nodded, her face an unmoving mask.

"It won't be easy to convince him to do the same thing," said Brooklyn.

An idea came to Annalisa. "We just need to make it, um, irr . . ."

"Irresistible," said Wheels. "Yeah, totally. He's all about the publicity, right? Tell him *Power Profiles* is coming to talk to you."

Power Profiles was a Discovery Channel show that profiled various parahumans around the country, with an emphasis on the sensational. The show's editors could make even the most mundane powers seem astonishing thanks to recreations of events, CGI effects, and exciting music. Annalisa had binge-watched most of the first two seasons over her last winter break and harbored a secret desire for them to do an episode on her.

Carson snapped his fingers. "We can make that happen, I think. One of the show's producers is a PRA agent. If we get the world to Chrétien that the show is coming here, it will force his hand and he'll act so they have something to cover. Give us a day to make some calls. By tomorrow, we should have a deadline in place."

Annalisa stepped forward. "Brittany, can you guys handle your end?"

"Yes." Brittany still didn't move. "I promise."

Annalisa extended her hand. "I promise that the Neighborhood Watch will be there to back you up." She remembered a phrase from *Rooftops*. She'd liked the sound of it the first time she heard it, and this seemed like the best time to repeat it. "Justice will prevail."

Brittany looked at her and her lips twitched, just for a moment, as if she'd almost smiled. Instead, she nodded, her gaze meeting Annalisa's. "Yes, it will."

Chapter Twenty-Seven

A rapping on her window yanked Annalisa out of a sound sleep. She leaped into the air to hover over her bed, her fists cocked and ready to do battle with whatever intruder had picked the wrong house to burgle.

"Relax, Capitána. It's me."

The familiar voice coming from the shadow in the window, even muffled through the glass, gave Annalisa pause. She turned on her bedside lamp and saw Brittany Arnold's face through the window. The girl wore the last costume they'd designed, complete with the black scarf. Her hair was pulled into two braids and then coiled into knots up high on either side of her head. The whole effect, especially late at night, combined to give her an exotic look that said *superhero*.

"Turn off your light, stupid, before someone sees."

Annalisa turned off the light and opened her window. "Don't call me stupid. What are you doing here?"

"Can you come outside? So we can talk?"

"Yeah, just a minute. Let me get dressed." Annalisa wasn't about to go flying around the neighborhood in a ratty oversized Snoopy t-shirt and underwear. She found her jean shorts and slipped them on, then gathered up the bottom hem of the t-shirt in a hair tie so it would sit tight against her torso instead of flapping.

Then she grabbed her new cape and pulled it over her head. Her mom had made it for her the day before. She hadn't asked any more questions after Annalisa said she lost her first cape and that was one of the biggest reasons Annalisa loved her mom. The new cape was sewn to the collar and sleeves of a heavy-duty t-shirt so it wouldn't accidentally fall off, but she could still tear it off if she was in danger of having it get caught on something.

"Really? Another cape?" Brittany sounded disgusted.

"You wore your costume, I'm wearing mine. Now do you want me to come out or can I go back to bed?"

"Sorry. It's just . . . yeah." Brittany moved aside so Annalisa could exit through the window.

"Where are we going?"

"Somewhere we can talk."

"Why now?"

"Because I need to go over it all while it's still fresh in my mind."

Annalisa grabbed her phone so she could take notes and then followed Brittany out into the night sky. The air was strangely layered between warm and cool, moist and dry, as they gained altitude. Flying at night was something Annalisa hadn't done often, and although it wasn't scary, it was exhilarating to know she was essentially invisible. They flew onward until a skeletal building structure appeared out of the darkness and Annalisa realized they'd come to the building her father's company was helping to build, where she'd taken Carson to question him and where she'd first found the armored truck guards tied up.

They flew up to the incomplete roof and sat at the edge, feet dangling over a drop of several stories. A warm evening breeze made Annalisa's hair and cape flutter as she looked over at Brittany. The other girl stared out at the lights of Loveland, overshadowed by the great swell of the mountains to the west and the wisps of clouds high enough to still be lit by the long-set sun.

"Okay, we're here. What's on your mind, Britt?"

Brittany flashed a tight smile for a moment at her nickname—her *real* nickname, the one her father had given her. "Did you bring your phone?"

Annalisa nodded.

"Get it out. We talked *L'imposteur* into another robbery. I put all the details on my phone."

Annalisa pulled her phone from her back pocket. "He said he's going to do another robbery?"

"Well, no. But he never said he was going to the first time, either. He said he knew someone who could do it, who was willing to let us bust him. Then he could report on it and get us all the publicity. When he found out *Power Profiles* is coming to see us, we barely had to convince him at all."

"So what's his plan? When's it all going down."

"He didn't tell us his plan. He just said where we needed to be and when. Friday, just before five P.M."

"*This* Friday?" Annalisa's heart skipped a beat. "That's the day after tomorrow!"

"No, it's tomorrow. It's already Thursday."

"But that doesn't give us enough time!"

Brittany shrugged. "It's what we've got. That's why I came and got you now. I figure we'll need every minute between now and then."

"You don't know what his plan is? You don't know how he's going to rob the bank?"

"Nope. He just said we should be getting ice cream at the Baskin's near the bank and that's how we'll be in the area. He said we'll know what to do." She sniffed. "We've spent our lives training for this."

Annalisa touched her phone to Brittany's, and it beeped to let her know the file had transferred. She looked at the screen and saw a new icon on her screen. "I guess I better go read this and start sharing it with the rest of the team." She floated off the edge of the building.

"Before you go, I want to say something."

Annalisa turned back to look at Brittany. "Okay, what?"

"That man killed my father. He's not going to go to Deep Six. Or back to France."

"Why not?"

Brittany floated off the edge of the building herself to hover over Annalisa, an inky shadow blotting out the stars overhead. "Because I'm going to kill him. And you're going to keep your team out of my way, or else."

Annalisa crossed her arms. This was familiar territory, Brittany making wild threats and bullying. "Or else what?"

"Or else I'll be your enemy forever." Brittany launched herself up and back, heeling over in a barrel roll until she was flying away from Annalisa like a bullet from the barrel of a gun.

Annalisa made a halfhearted attempt to follow after her, but Brittany could fly faster, and she didn't want to be caught. Her venomous admission was worrying at Annalisa like a dog at a bone, and she felt like she needed to talk it over with someone. Her first thought was to go visit Breezy, not just because maybe he *liked* her, but because he was in many ways the soul of the Neighborhood Watch. His easygoing attitude and ready willingness to overlook slights perceived or actual, errors in judgment, or even poor intentions was like the glue that kept the wildly different personalities of the team together. Also, Annalisa liked his short dreads and the way he laughed, but that wasn't going to help her stop Brittany from committing a terrible crime.

No, she had to go back to where it all began, to the one person who understood more about being a superhero and what it meant than anyone else in the Neighborhood Watch.

She flew to Wheels' house.

The auto salvage yard was quietly frightening in the darkness. The crushed and stacked cars looked like monsters frozen in time, their shattered grills looming like mouths, waiting to devour an unwary passerby. The only sound Annalisa could hear as she came down beside their headquarters was the quiet hum of a nearby transformer and crickets chirping. Some tiny creature nearby met its end with a squeak that cut off suddenly, and the silent shadow of an owl cruised up and over the wall of automobiles.

Goosebumps rose up and down Annalisa's arms and legs, even though the still air was still stuffy and warm from the daytime heat. She tried to tell herself that she was tough, and strong, and a parahuman, and she shouldn't be afraid of the dark, but when she heard the rustling of some predator—maybe just a cat, maybe a demon from the nether world—as it scrambled after a rodent, she lost all sense of bravado and flew across the yard to the house and knocked on Wheels' window. "Wheels. Wheels! Aighleigh, let me in!" she whisper-shouted.

Wheels' bedside lamp illuminated. The girl lay in her bed with a tablet computer on her belly, her brown hair sticking out in cowlicks all over. She saw Annalisa at the window and raised her tablet.

One swipe of her finger tilted her bed up so she could see better. Another unlocked the window, and a third brought her chair rolling over beside the bed so she could board it if needed. "

"Annalisa? What's wrong?" Wheels set her tablet aside, but still kept it in easy reach.

Annalisa paused, but Wheels would understand. "It's scary out here."

The window slid open. "Yeah, it is." Wheels yawned. "Why are you out here in the middle of the night? I was dreaming about running."

"Oh. I'm sorry." Annalisa felt like a wet blanket for interrupting something like that.

"It's okay. I'm always designing legs. Someday I'll make myself a really good pair, and then I'll run everywhere. I can do it. All I need is time. And maybe a 3-D printer. And a couple of Jet Propulsion Lab-grade gyroscopes." She sighed. "Actually, there are a lot of things I need. But someday I'll do it."

"I believe you," Annalisa said. "And I'll be the first one to race you."

Wheels smiled. "You'll lose. But why are you here?"

"It's Brittany. She told me that *L'imposteur* is going to hit a bank Friday just before closing. She gave me the details." Annalisa held up her phone. Wheels touched it with her tablet to transfer the file.

"So we've got our work cut out for us. Good thing we only have a half day today, and it's Field Day. Not like I'll be doing a lot of running around. I can start planning."

"There's more. It's Brittany. I . . . I think she's going to kill him."

Wheels' eyes widened. "What? She can't! I mean, she's just a kid like us."

"Of course she can. All she has to do is hit him hard enough. Or break him in half. Or throw him against something really hard. Or drop something heavy on him."

"God, Annalisa, stop it already! That's gross!"

"It's true. If she wants to kill him, it's going to be very hard to stop her."

"He does kind of deserve to die. He murdered their father."

"That doesn't make it okay to kill him. That's not what Just Cause would do. Or Breezy."

Wheels nodded. "Yeah, he'd tell us we need to be better than that."

"And we do. We have to be the real heroes. Maybe we don't get the publicity or recognition that the triplets do, but we have to do things the right way. And that means we can't let Brittany— or either of her sisters—kill *L'imposteur.*"

Wheels pushed her hair out of her face. "So we not only have to stop him after he robs the bank but before he gets away, but then we have to protect him from the Culture Club? You're spreading us awfully thin. If we're not careful, the whole thing will blow up in our faces."

"Then we'll have to be careful, and have a good plan, too."

Wheels snickered. "No plan survives contact with the enemy. We're going to have to improvise a lot, and on the fly too."

"That's where you come in. I think you should be in charge of this."

"Why not you? This has been your project since the beginning."

Annalisa sighed. "You're better at thinking through problems than I am. I let my heart get in the way sometimes."

"That's important. You can't just be some kind of unthinking machine. All the feels are important too."

"So are the smarts, and you're smarter than me. Also, I want you to do it. When we first started the Neighborhood Watch, it was an equal partnership. Brains and brawn."

"I prefer Beauty and the Beast." Wheels winked. "But don't worry, I won't let anyone else call you *Beast*."

Annalisa laughed, and then covered her mouth so she wouldn't be too loud and awaken Wheels' dad.

"Go home, Annalisa. Get some sleep. You're going to need it. This afternoon, we'll work out our plan. Then tomorrow, we're going to bust a real live supervillain."

Chapter Twenty-Eight

The bank was hot and stuffy, and Annalisa had nervous sweat trickling down her back between her shoulder blades. She was in disguise, with her hair pulled back in a ponytail and one of her father's baseball caps pulled down low on her forehead. She had loitered outside until Wheels reported that *L'imposteur* was on the move, at which point she and Hothead had gone into the bank with Torvald. He looked very little like a librarian in his button down shirt, tie, and jacket. He looked more like a typical young urban professional, ready to get some money out for playing on the weekend. While he stood in line, Annalisa and Cole sat in the chairs by the front doors and pretended to read magazines. Cole had a lightweight track suit on over his costume, while Annalisa's costume looked so much like regular clothing, all she'd had to do was carefully roll up her cape and tuck it into her back pocket. The lump of it pressing against her was a gentle reminder that they were there to be superheroes.

Both teams—the Neighborhood Watch *and* the Culture Club—were carefully placed at strategic locations around the bank in preparation for the plan they'd hastily thrown together. The triplets were sitting at a table inside the Baskin Robbins across the street, letting their ice cream cups melt into soup while they watched the front of the bank. Breezy was lurking on the roof of the Mexican restaurant at the other end of the parking lot. He could watch the bank from his vantage point, but his mission was far more important. If the Culture Club got out of control, his job was to use his powers to stop them. "How are you going to do that?" Annalisa asked him. "There are three of them and only one of you."

"Subtraction, yo," was all he said, and wouldn't expand upon it further.

Rascal was hanging around in front of the ice cream shop, likewise out of costume, doing skateboard tricks with a couple older kids. Wheels was back at the Neighborhood Watch HQ with all her monitor gear running, along with six scavenged swamp coolers running at full blast to keep the inside of the Winnebago cool and to keep her gear from melting. Carson was with her, coordinating with the local police and the two representatives from Deep Six waiting on standby. They had flown in earlier in the day at the behest of the PRA and were prepared to accept a wily and dangerous parahuman into their midst.

Annalisa's and Cole's phones buzzed, and they each pulled them out to look. It was a picture from Wheels, showing *L'imposteur* behind the wheel of a nondescript silver sedan. He was wearing a jacket and tie, looking honestly like half the men in line in the bank. It would be a great disguise should he have to blend in anywhere. His face was transformed into a bland version of Carson's, less defined around the jaw, with some puffiness around the eyes, that made him look older and somewhat less threatening. Wheels was following his car with one of her drones, and she sent regular pictures and updates to the others.

Rascal picked up when *L'imposteur* pulled into the bank parking lot and left his car. He snapped a picture of the man and of the car's license plate and sent it to the group. *Here he comes*, texted the skateboarder. Torvald, in line with three people in front of him, casually checked his phone and glanced back as the bank door opened.

L'imposteur strolled in, carrying a black briefcase and tucking his sunglasses into his jacket parker as he strolled across the floor. His face looking like a swollen Carson's was enough to make Annalisa look twice to be sure it was their quarry after all. Instead of getting in line, he looked over the personal bankers at their desks, then chose one and walked directly over to him. The man smiled at him. "Hi, how can I help you?"

Annalisa strained to overhear him say, "Hello, I'd like to see my safe deposit box, please." He held up the briefcase.

The bank nodded. "Of course, sir. Right this way."

Annalisa texted the group. Wheels responded to her almost immediately. *I can't access bank cameras. Use the dragonfly.*

The dragonfly was a special drone Wheels had built. It was shaped like its namesake and barely the size of Annalisa's hand. She pulled it from her pocket. It was built from cell phone parts, including a camera, battery, and even the wings were made from the clear screen covers. Tiny motors operated the drone's wings. According to Wheels, it only had an eight minute battery life, but she could control it through Bluetooth via an app she'd set up on Annalisa's phone. Most importantly of all, it was only about as loud as a buzzing fly, and with the general hubbub inside the bank, that sound would be lost. Annalisa pushed the wings into their slots until they clicked, then opened the app on her phone. It established a Bluetooth connection with the drone in her lap, and then logged into a secure server back in the Neighborhood Watch headquarters. A previously dark window on the screen illuminated, showing a wide-angle view of Annalisa and Cole, staring down at the drone in wide-eyed wonder.

The drone buzzed to life in Annalisa's lap, its wings moving like a hummingbird's. It lifted off, spun around once to get its bearings, and then zipped toward the back of the bank, flying low. Maybe in a previous age, people might have noticed it, but all the people in line were all staring at their phones.

Cole leaned in next to Annalisa to watch the whirling video feed from the drone as it whipped around the banker desks then up and over the half-height door separating the teller counter from the rest of the bank. One teller squeaked in surprise, making Annalisa and Cole look up quickly to see if they'd been caught. A young man with glasses and shoulder-length hair pulled up into a ponytail at the back of his head asked what was wrong, and the teller said she just saw the biggest dragonfly ever. They laughed and went back to work.

The drone flew through the vault entrance, showing them a glimpse of tall lockers that Annalisa thought probably held the bank's cash reserves. Movies had taught her there should be a table with a big stack of cash on it, but the only money she saw was in one of the lockers that was open. Still, it ignited a small streak of avarice in her and she wondered what she and the rest of the

Neighborhood Watch could do with a big pile of cash. They could upgrade their headquarters until it looked more like something that the Culture Club had. They could all get custom-made costumes that made them look both fearsome and heroic instead of like a group of kids who happened to have powers. In that moment she understood why some people turned to crime. It was a shortcut that, if it worked, could leave the robber set up for life.

On the other hand, it only took one mistake to get caught, and *L'imposteur* was making that mistake.

"Look there," Cole whispered. The banker was lying on the floor in the safe deposit box room adjacent to the main vault. *L'imposteur* must have slugged him. He'd already taken the banker's jacket. As Annalisa and Cole watched in horror, *L'imposteur*'s face flowed like claymation to match the banker's face. *L'imposteur* searched the man's pockets, then dragged him beneath the table. He popped open the briefcase, which was empty but for a handful of keys. He used the keys from his briefcase and the banker's key to open several safe deposit boxes, removed their contents, and dumped them into his briefcase. Then he noticed the drone where it sat, looking at him from the corner of the room, and hurled one of the empty boxes at it, which was the last thing Annalisa and Cole saw on the screen.

Things were about to go down. Torvald was at the counter, showing the teller his badge and speaking to her in a low, urgent tone. Annalisa realized they had only seconds to get ready. There was a supervillain in the vault, who was maybe armed, and the bank was full of people. "Cole, we've got to get the civilians out of here," she whispered.

"How?"

"Scare them out." The two heroes of the Neighborhood Watch jumped to their feet. Annalisa yanked her cape out of her back pocket. It unfurled like a banner as she threw away her hat and shook out her hair. Beside her, Cole tore open his track suit like a comic book superhero, showing the flame logo on his costume beneath it. It looked so heroic and he was so proud of it in that moment that Annalisa feared his powers might completely desert him, so she tripped him. He fell over his breakaway pants and hit the carpet face-first.

"Ow!" he yelped, and his hair ignited like someone had thrown a match into dry grass.

Annalisa felt a tremendous stab of guilt race through her, not only for what she'd just done to her teammate, but what she was about to do. She needed him furious, for that was the only way he'd truly scare away the civilians. She grabbed him by his costume top and lifted him until she was only inches away from his face. His eyebrows were smoldering and his face was bright red. The anger was coming. "Is that the best you can do? You're pathetic." She threw him toward the teller counter. He rolled and bounced past the line of shocked civilians until he stopped beside the counter.

He roared in incoherent fury, and *his entire body caught flame.*

Chapter Twenty-Nine

If the bank customers had been concerned before, the human torch was enough to send them running screaming for the doors. Torvald gasped in surprise and jumped back from the sudden wave of heat.

"Torvald, go! We've got this!" Annalisa shouted as she flew past the fleeing civilians to land beside Hothead. Torvald hesitated for a moment, but even a PRA agent could be spooked by unknown powers, and nothing in anyone's reports suggested Hothead had the capability of complete flammability. He ran after the civilians.

Hothead didn't appear to be in any discomfort. He held up his arms and looked at himself in astonishment. "Whoa."

"Are you all right?" Annalisa spotted a fire extinguisher on one wall and edged in that direction.

"Yeah, I'm good. This is intense! Go get that guy, Capitána! Uh oh . . ." Hothead noticed the carpet around his feet was smoldering and he ran across the lobby to stand on the slab of granite floor by the entrance. "I just need to . . ." He trailed off as he focused on controlling his power.

Annalisa flew over the teller counter to the vault entrance, her fists cocked, ready to knock *L'imposteur* out once again. "Arnold, or Chrétien, or whatever your name is, this is the Neighborhood Watch. Come out with your hands up or I'm coming in to get you." When there was no response, she added, "I'm counting to three and then coming in. One . . . two . . ."

The bank's sprinkler system erupted, spraying water in all directions and thoroughly dousing Hothead's flames in a burst of steam.

Soaked through to the skin, Annalisa poked her head around the edge of the vault to look for Chrétien, but the only person in the vault was the unconscious banker. Somehow, *L'imposteur* had managed to sneak out in the chaos after Hothead burst into flame.

He was out!

She whipped out her phone and hit the emergency broadcast button on the Neighborhood Watch app. "Capitána here. *L'imposteur* somehow got out of the bank with everyone else." She was going to describe him but then realized that would be wasted effort. Then she remembered something he wouldn't have left without. "Briefcase. He's got a big black briefcase."

"I got him," said Rascal over her phone. "He's in the parking lot with everyone else."

"I see him too," said Breezy. "Hey, wait! Stop!"

A noisy commotion commenced outside the bank and Annalisa had a sinking feeling she knew exactly what had happened. She flew past Hothead at top speed and burst out of the bank through the glass doors. They shattered into a thousand pieces as she emerged into the afternoon sun.

Breezy was fighting a pitched battle with the Culture Club, blasting the front of the ice cream store with as strong a gale as he could manage. The chairs and tables out front were all overturned from his winds. Brooklyn had one arm wrapped several times around a light pole to keep from being tossed aside and her other arm around Brianna, who probably couldn't focus enough to use her powers as wind bludgeoned her. Brittany, though, was pushing her way through, and Annalisa was afraid for Breezy if she reached him.

Rascal had stuck his mask to his face and was skating across the street, keeping low out of Breezy's line of fire. A police car screeched to a halt in front of the bank. The driver never saw Rascal, but the daredevil skateboarder wasn't fazed. He kicked his board beneath the cruiser, rolled across the hood, and landed back on his board once again. He saw Annalisa and pointed toward a couple of men getting into a car at one end of the parking lot. They both looked familiar and Annalisa realized they *both* looked like Torvald.

The car's engine roared and it peeled out of the parking lot, tearing across the grassy easement onto the main road. Annalisa raised her phone. "This is Capitána. *L'imposteur* has a hostage. It's Torvald. I'm in pursuit." She tucked her phone into her back pocket, hoping it wouldn't be damaged by her wet clothes, and flew after the fleeing car. Two police cars joined the chase behind her but it looked like Annalisa was the only one who had any chance of catching the car.

The car tore through an intersection against the light to the blaring of horns and screeching of tires. Annalisa followed right behind it, keeping the car in her sights but keeping her distance because of Torvald. She couldn't tell whether he was driving or *L'imposteur* was, but either way, she didn't want to risk hurting them.

She might not have a choice, she realized, as the car sideswiped a truck that didn't get out of the way quick enough. Civilians were going to get hurt if she didn't bring the chase to an end quickly.

"Out of my way!" a voice screamed behind her, and Annalisa knew Breezy hadn't been able to hold back Brittany any longer.

Brittany shoved past Annalisa, flying lower and lower, and Annalisa thought she was probably going to try to wreck the car with Torvald in it. She grabbed onto Brittany. "No, don't!"

Brittany punched her in the face.

Annalisa gasped as stars flashed in her vision, but she held onto Brittany. "Don't!" she repeated. "Torvald's in there."

"*I don't care!*" screamed Brittany.

Beneath them, the car skidded around a corner, sending one of its hubcaps flying through the front window of a restaurant.

"We have to stop it before someone gets hurt!" Annalisa wrestled with Brittany in midair, but didn't have the hand-to-hand fighting skills that the Arnold sister did. Between the personal trainers Sujin and Marek, Brittany was an accomplished fighter. She elbowed Annalisa in the belly, driving the air out of her lungs. As Annalisa struggled to inhale, the two girls crashed through a billboard.

The momentary distraction allowed Annalisa to take her cape and wrap it around Brittany's face. She didn't want to punch the other girl, especially when she was already blinded, so she settled for flinging Brittany back behind her. Brittany tumbled head over heels as Annalisa went after the fleeing car once more. A glance back over her shoulder showed that Brittany recovered quickly and Annalisa saw murder in the girl's eyes, but she saw something else as well that gave her hope: Breezy's big blue cape.

The boy had whipped up a veritable chinook, and his cape was dragging him through the skies like a balloon in a gale. He twisted as if he was the ornament on the tail of a kite and Annalisa couldn't imagine how dizzy that would make her. If he caught up to Brittany, or even just got close to her, he might distract her enough for Annalisa to stop the car safely without someone getting hurt.

Road traffic was thinning out as the local police got ahead of the pursuit and started blocking roads. Annalisa noticed traffic lights were stuck showing nothing but green lights for the fleeing car with red lights in all the other directions. At first, she thought *L'imposteur* must have somehow hacked the system, but then she realized it was probably Wheels. By keeping the lights red, it would minimize the chances of the fleeing car crashing into some other vehicle.

Annalisa dropped down low behind the sedan, knowing she only had one chance to bring it to a stop, and prepared to grab hold of it.

An inattentive truck driver ran a red light and his truck barreled into the side of the fleeing sedan, narrowly missing Annalisa. It spun around sideways and vaulted into the air. Without thinking, she dove underneath it and caught it as it tumbled before it could crash onto its roof. With a Herculean effort, she halted the momentum of the vehicle's wild roll and then heaved it back over onto its wheels. All four of them snapped off when it hit the ground, and Annalisa peered inside, fearing the worst.

Chapter Thirty

The two Torvalds inside the car were both shaking their heads and bleeding from cuts on their faces and hands. Annalisa couldn't tell them apart—not even by their clothing, since their outfits were virtually identical thanks to the bland professional attire both had worn. She had to tear the seatbelt off the first man because it wouldn't unlatch. She carefully lifted him out as the pursuing police cars skidded to a halt and the officers within tumbled out, sidearms drawn.

Brittany hit the ground on the other side of the car, wrenched the ruined door off its hinges, and lifted the other man free of the wreck.

"Brittany, don't!" cried Annalisa as the other girl drew back a fist to pummel the dazed Torvald. "Look at his face!"

Brittany hesitated, looking at the face of the man she held, and then looking over at the one Annalisa had. "They . . . they're the same. Which one is it?" She shook the man she held. "Who are you?"

"T-Torvald," said the man.

"No, *I'm* Torvald," said the one Annalisa held. "He asked my name when he took me hostage."

"Girls, release those men and step back," one of the policemen ordered.

"Can't do that, officers." Annalisa tried to sound as official as possible. "One of these men is a federal agent and the other is a dangerous criminal. We have to figure out which is which."

Brittany set her Torvald down next to Annalisa's. "Which of you is the real Torvald?"

"I am," said both men.

"Dang it," Annalisa muttered. "They look exactly alike."

"Get one of them to tell you something only he would know," said Brittany.

"Like what?"

"I don't know!" Brittany stamped her foot on the pavement hard enough to crack it.

"Girls, this is your last warning." The policemen fanned out around them, cutting off escape routes for the two Torvalds, keeping their weapons aimed at the two potential suspects. "Step away from the suspects."

"They can fly," said another cop.

"I don't care if they can turn into hummingbirds," said the first. "Get clear."

A police SUV screeched to a halt and officers Bickle and Velez jumped out. Annalisa glanced back at them. "Bick! Evie! Tell them to back off. We don't know what other powers the impostor has."

Another officer spoke up. "Just heard from Dispatch. They say the PRA and Deep Six representatives are en route. Should be here in just a few minutes."

"You hear that?" said Annalisa. "One of you guys is going to a deep, dark hole in the ground."

"Yeah, but which one?" Brittany was flexing her fingers like she was ready to crush both men into paste. Her indecision was the only thing holding her back.

Another person got out of Bickle and Velez' SUV. It was Carson. A look of relief crossed the faces of both Torvalds. Annalisa wondered if *L'imposteur* knew Carson and Torvald were married. From the identical reactions of both men, either he knew or he was very good at mimicking the reactions of others. She suspected it was the latter.

Carson raised his badge to the officers. "I'm Special Agent Carson of the Parahuman Resources Agency. I'll determine which of these men is your suspect and which is my partner in just a moment, if you'll lower your weapons." He smiled. "Don't want to accidentally get shot."

"Do as he says," said Bickle.

The police lowered their weapons but kept them in their hands. Carson stepped up to the two Torvalds. "I'm going to ask each of you one question, and you can whisper the response in my ear. Girls, watch them close."

"No funny business," Brittany warned. "Or I'll hit you so hard that when you wake up, your clothes will be out of style."

Carson took the first Torvald's head in his hands with solemn, deliberate movements, and delivered a passionate kiss on the lips. Then he whispered something to the first Torvald and turned his head so he could listen to the response. Whatever that Torvald said made him smile. He nodded his acknowledgement to the first and turned to the second. Another kiss, another whispering in the ear. The second Torvald looked positively scandalized at whatever Carson had said to him. "I can't believe you asked me that," he said.

Annalisa tensed, ready to act. It looked to her like the second Torvald was stalling for time. Maybe he was trying to figure out the correct response. Carson had looked pretty satisfied with the first one's answer. Had he already figured it out?

"Tell me," Carson said.

"Fine, I will." The second Torvald spoke through clenched teeth, then he wilted. "Come on, ask me anything else. Anything at all. Just not that."

"It's him, can't you see?" shouted the first Torvald. "He's stalling for time. He doesn't know."

"You don't know what he asked me," retorted the second Torvald. "And if you were me, you'd be embarrassed about it too. I can't believe you kissed him like that."

"Why wouldn't I? *I'm married to him!*" screamed the first Torvald.

"*Sugarbumps!*" the second Torvald shouted. "That's your pet name for me, *and I hate it!*"

A couple of the police officers burst out laughing.

Carson stepped back and smiled, then pointed at the first Torvald. "Officers, arrest that man."

The first Torvald's face flowed into Gérard Chrétien's as he yanked something from the back of his pants and pointed it at Carson.

"*Gun! Gun!*" shouted Officer Velez.

Annalisa didn't even think. She jumped between Carson and Chrétien as the latter pulled the trigger. Something punched her in the side harder than she'd ever been hit in her life. The roar of the pistol deafened her as the stink of gunpowder washed over her. She bounced against Carson, forgot how to fly, and fell. He caught her just as she saw Brittany clap her hands over Chrétien's gun hand, crushing all his fingers as she crushed the pistol inside of them. His scream was short-lived, as she followed up with a heavy uppercut that lifted him all the way off the ground. He was unconscious before he hit the ground.

"*Annalisa!*" Carson's shout seemed to come from a long way off through the ringing in Annalisa's ears.

With a fluttering of blue, Breezy landed beside them, tears in his eyes. "Is she shot? Is she hurt? You got to get her to a doctor, man. Lemme do it!"

"No, let me. I'm faster," said Brittany.

Annalisa felt her side. It was sore, but somehow she thought being shot would be a lot worse. She raised her hand up. There wasn't even a speck of blood. "Wait—" She coughed, trying to regain her breath. "I think . . . I think I'm okay." She pulled up her shirt enough so everyone could see her side. As she did so, a flattened piece of metal fell out and hit the pavement. There was a nasty-looking welt on her skin but no blood.

Breezy picked up the thing that had fallen. "Yo, ain't this a bullet? You're bulletproof? Why didn't you say so?"

Annalisa wanted to say she hadn't known, which was the truth. Her reaction to the gun had been instinctual: protect the innocent, even at risk to oneself. The only thought in her mind at that moment had been to save Carson, no matter what.

It was a hero's instinct.

Chapter Thirty-One

Things happened very quickly following the arrest of Gérard Chrétien. He was charged with robbery, assault, kidnapping, attempted murder, and the two Deep Six officers delighted in letting him know what kind of gourmet turkey he'd be getting fed down in the hole while awaiting his trial.

Carson and Torvald were recalled to Washington DC to report on the events in the sleepy little town of Loveland, Colorado. Before they left, both men took the time to visit the Neighborhood Watch in their headquarters and thank them for their efforts in helping catch a wanted felon. "He would have gotten away with it, too, if it wasn't for you kids."

"Ain't we supposed to have a stupid dog, too?" Breezy asked, and everyone laughed.

Carson shook Annalisa's hand. "You saved my life. I'm very grateful for that, Annalisa. Your actions will figure prominently in my report." He looked up. "All of you will. The Neighborhood Watch is everything a superhero team ought to be, and we're very proud of you."

"Thanks, you guys, for not making Carson a widow," said Torvald.

"You're welcome," said Annalisa.

"Sugarbumps," added Rascal, which set everyone off in gales of laughter again.

The police sent officers Bickle and Velez around to present the Neighborhood Watch with a special commendation from the Chief of Police, and they mentioned the Mayor was probably going to have them over so she could shake their hands. Wheels said they'd do their best to fit the Mayor into their schedule. Suddenly all the attention which had originally been intended to focus upon the Culture Club was zeroed in on the Neighborhood Watch, and they had become celebrities. They'd already even had preliminary contact from *Power Profiles*.

As far as the Culture Club went, Annalisa only got to see them one more time. The three girls met her atop the building under construction once more. "We're moving away," said Brooklyn without preamble. "Mom said this town isn't big enough for two teenage superhero teams."

"Plus she wants to work on her BASH brand," said Brianna. "High fashion means New York."

"You're going to be right there," said Annalisa. "Just Cause New York. That's the main team. You're going to be around them all the time. I wish I could be. I'm jealous."

"We'll be back. Eighth grade at whatever school Mom picks out and then it's the Hero Academy down in Denver," said Brianna.

"Unless we decide to chuck it all and be supervillains," said Brooklyn. "That's an option."

"Listen, Annalisa, I need to tell you something." Brittany had been uncharacteristically quiet up to that point. "Thanks for helping to keep me from making the big mistake."

"Big mistake?" asked Annalisa.

"I wanted to kill Chrétien. I mean, really, really bad. After I crushed his gun hand, I was going to punch his stupid face right off his skull, but you said *don't*."

Annalisa laughed. "I couldn't have said that. I just got shot. It knocked my breath out."

Brittany shrugged. "Whether you really said it or I heard it in my mind, it was your voice, and it stopped me." She extended her hand to Annalisa. "You're a better superhero than me."

Annalisa shook Brittany's hand. "It's not a competition. It's just about doing the right thing when you can."

"I'll try to be better. We all will." Brittany gathered up her sisters. "We'll see you at the Academy, Capitána."

They flew away.

Annalisa flew home.

Her mother met her at the door. "There you are, you little troublemaker. Why haven't you been answering your phone?"

Annalisa felt a wave of guilt wash over her. "I think, uh, I forgot to charge it. *Lo siento*, Mamá."

"Well, never mind that. Come inside. You have a visitor." Her mother stepped aside.

Annalisa entered the front room, and there she was, sitting on the couch. She would have recognized that costume anywhere. Gold boots and gloves and belt. Goggles. Crimson bodysuit. Horseshoes on her hips and a horse logo on her chest. *Mustang Sally!*

Mustang Sally stood immediately and walked over to Annalisa. She was much shorter than Annalisa had expected—shorter even than her mother. She shook Annalisa's hand and smiled. "La Capitána. I'm very pleased to meet you. I've heard some amazing things about your team here and thought I'd come out to introduce myself."

Annalisa's tongue was frozen solid in her mouth. Meeting her personal hero was something she'd never considered could actually happen to her.

"She's a big fan," said Annalisa's father. "She has your picture up over her bed."

Mustang Sally smiled. "Well, I'm a big fan of her too. Anyone who puts together a team of superheroes—of *any* age—and then proceeds to do something as heroic as stopping a crime and preventing people from getting hurt . . . Well, that's why we exist. It's why we do what we do."

"I—" Annalisa began, and then stopped, ashamed of herself.

"What is it, Capitána?" asked Mustang Sally.

"I . . . I mean, do you . . . think I could be on Just Cause with you? Someday?"

Mustang Sally smiled. "I would like that very much. Believe me, I'll be watching your progress very closely throughout your time at the Academy. I think you'd be a fine addition to Just Cause New York. Now then . . ." She pulled her goggles from her forehead down over her eyes. "I believe you have some teammates I need to meet. Shall we let them know we're coming?"

Annalisa pulled out her phone. True to what she'd said to her mother, she'd neglected to charge it. As she watched, it dropped from three percent to flash the battery icon once and then shut off. "No," she said. "Let's surprise them."

ABOUT THE AUTHOR

Ian Thomas Healy dabbles in many different genres. He's a ten-time participant and winner of National Novel Writing Month and is also the creator of the *Writing Better Action Through Cinematic Techniques* workshop, which helps writers to improve their action scenes.

When not writing, which is rare, he enjoys watching hockey, reading comic books (and serious books, too), and living in the great state of Colorado, which he shares with his wife, children, house-pets, and approximately five million other people.

Visit www.ianthealy.com for more information.